Further Praise for *Starting Over*:

"A collection that stands as a reintroduction to the work of an important American writer. . . . Spencer concentrates on questions of sex and class and secrecy, and the emotional geography she charts is never an easy one. Elliptical and at times astringent, she knows exactly how ruthless a family can be, and how quickly the self may splinter. . . . 'Return Trip' and 'The Wedding Visitor' stand among her best, and so does an understated bit of Gothic called 'On the Hill,' a tale that both invites and resists explanation." —Michael Gorra, *New York Review of Books*

"[Spencer] is, by any measure, a master of the form, and the stories in *Starting Over* show all the deftness and insight for which she has long been known. . . . One of the chief pleasures of these stories is Spencer's sly and delicate style. Her prose is feather-light, free of even a single spare word but filled with meaning and wit. . . . Spencer's voice has been a quiet treasure of the American literary scene for more than sixty years, and the stories in *Starting Over* are as sharp and powerful as any she has written." —Maria Browning, Chapter 16

"Spencer has been storytelling in full frontal view of Literature, in tandem with a cast of immortals. . . . Few Americans have written so insistently and piercingly about the paradox of family, the myriad ways in which the force that sustains is also the force that erodes. Her new story collection, *Starting Over*—her first book in thirteen years—continues her peerless articulation of the intimate rhythms in Southern existence. . . . Every now and again the empty cosmos gets it right: that we have a healthy Spencer still witnessing at the age of ninety-two is a fact of flesh that feels more like a gift of grace, and *Starting Over* is a

numinous addition to the catalog of an American treasure."
—William Giraldi, *Oxford American*

"[Spencer] is, as she ever was, one of America's best short story writers, with her invention and craft undimmed. Next time they bring out Spencer's *Selected Fiction* they will have to wedge in at least two more masterpieces from *Starting Over*. . . . Spencer's body of work—her short stories more in vogue than her novels, but that may turn around with time and fashion—is a lasting contribution to the permanent national shelf."
—Wilton Barnhardt, *Slate*

"A collection to celebrate. . . . The good, old short story in the hands of master writer Elizabeth Spencer still occupies a seemingly boundless imaginative terrain."
—Steve Yates, *Clarion-Ledger*

"Ms. Spencer, 92, is mostly concerned here with familial entanglements and loose ends. . . . [Her] Southern world may be blemished, but she approaches it with considerable sympathy."
—John Williams, *New York Times*

"Now in her 10th decade, Elizabeth Spencer breaks all the old rules if she has to about how to tell a story, shifting points of view, inserting flashbacks in the middle of a fragile tale about the present in order to get at a necessary and beautifully revealed truth about the past. Its relation to the present. And as she puts it, the whole flawed fabric of human relations."
—Alan Cheuse, *All Things Considered*

"Spencer [is] an elegant and subtle writer. . . . Like Chekhov, the moments of most acute misery—those achingly common things that nearly kill us all—are offstage. . . . There are nine stories here, all wonderful, subtle and complex—which makes the cumulative effect all the more alarming." —Ann Beattie, *San Francisco Chronicle*

"*Starting Over* is a veritable Whitman's sampler of bite-sized stories stitched together by their shared stillness. . . . Spencer's stories dance with the illusion of happiness but swell with unspoken sadness. Humor bubbles to the surface in the most unexpected ways . . . but that humor, too, is fragile." —Michelle Moriarity Witt, *Charlotte Observer*

"*Starting Over*, the sixth and latest collection of stories in the long career of Chapel Hill author Elizabeth Spencer, is a master class in narrative economy. . . . [It's] the season of Spencer, a literary light in the Carolina Piedmont." —David Fellerath, *Indy Week*

"There seems to be nothing this extraordinary writer can't do. . . . Spencer recounts the details and doings of her characters in such spare, unfussy, almost conversational prose that she sounds at first like nothing so much as a shrewd family storyteller. . . . Spencer's great gift is her ability to take ordinariness and turn it inside out, to find focus in a muddle. . . . [D]azzling . . . 'On the Hill' might have been written by Hawthorne or Cheever—a work of genius, in other words. . . . Elizabeth Spencer seems to have spent her life watching, observing, always paying close attention, and for her it's the whole truth or nothing. As far as I can tell, she never missed a thing. Judging from the stories in her latest collection, she's not about to start now." —Malcolm Jones, *New York Times Book Review*

"I'm glad I can respond to Spencer's new collection of stories, *Starting Over*, like most human beings—just enjoy them as suspenseful, surprising reminders of how we live, how we relate to others and to ourselves. . . . What a pleasure to not have to work at reading, seeing, hearing, knowing. To be a part of the art. You don't have to be a writer to love these stories, but if you are, you will love them as you learn how it's done." —Clyde Edgerton, *Garden and Gun*

"Compelling. . . . [S]o many of the stories here are timeless, or more accurately ageless, domestic dramas that unfold in a recognizable but subtle world. . . . What we are hearing is the voice of experience, a description of how to be a survivor, which is a sensibility these characters and their author share." —David Ulin, *Los Angeles Times*

"Spencer's elegant stories are more about what doesn't happen than what does. . . . Quiet and spare prose ferries tiny but explosive clues which point to powerful insights lurking between the lines. . . . In Spencer's world, the emotional debt ceiling is always on the rise."
—*Kirkus Reviews*

"Spencer's first work of fiction, a novel titled *Fire in the Morning*, was published in 1948, and, as affirmed by her new collection of short fiction, these many years have not dulled the sharpness of her prose nor inched her into out-of-date perceptions of the world. Grand dame of southern letters that Spencer is, she remains a vital, passionate, contemporary-issues writer. [These stories show] the control and ease of a master; each story has superb qualities of artistry and social relevance." —Brad Hooper, *Booklist*, starred review

"Spencer has a special gift for the nuances in 'ordinary' human relationships; she creates suspense via anticipation more through interactions themselves. . . . Spencer's strength lies in highlighting human truths in captured moments." —*Publishers Weekly*

Also by Elizabeth Spencer

Novels:
The Night Travellers
The Salt Line
The Snare
No Place for an Angel
Knights and Dragons
The Light in the Piazza
The Voice at the Back Door
This Crooked Way
Fire in the Morning

Story Collections:
The Southern Woman
On the Gulf
Jack of Diamonds and Other Stories
Marilee
Ship Island and Other Stories

Memoir:
Landscapes of the Heart

Elizabeth Spencer

Starting Over

◆ STORIES ◆

LIVERIGHT PUBLISHING CORPORATION

A Division of W. W. Norton & Company

New York · London

For Allan Gurganus

For information about permission to reproduce selections from this book,
write to Permissions, Liveright Publishing Corporation,
a division of W. W. Norton & Company, Inc.,
500 Fifth Avenue, New York, NY 10110

For information about special discounts for bulk purchases, please contact
W. W. Norton Special Sales at specialsales@wwnorton.com or 800-233-4830

Manufacturing by Courier Westford
Book design by Ellen Cipriano
Production manager: Devon Zahn

Library of Congress Cataloging-in-Publication Data

Spencer, Elizabeth, 1921–
[Short stories. Selections]
Starting Over : Stories / Elizabeth Spencer. — First Edition.
pages cm
ISBN 978-0-87140-681-1 (hardcover)
I. Title.
PS3537.P4454A6 2014
813'.54—dc23

2013033483

ISBN 978-0-87140-298-1 pbk.

Liveright Publishing Corporation
500 Fifth Avenue, New York, N.Y. 10110
www.wwnorton.com

W. W. Norton & Company Ltd.
Castle House, 75/76 Wells Street, London W1T 3QT

1 2 3 4 5 6 7 8 9 0

Contents

◆ ◆ ◆

Starting Over

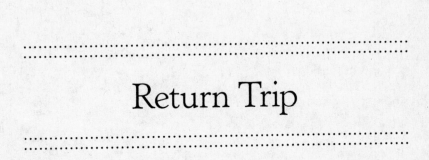

Return Trip

It was during a summer season Patricia and Boyd were spending together in the North Carolina mountains that Edward reappeared. He left a message on the answerphone predicting arrival the next afternoon, saying not to give a thought to driving into Asheville for him, that he would rent a car and come out, if at all welcome.

"At all welcome" sounded more than slightly aware that he might not be. Yet, of course, Patricia thought at once, they were going to say, "Come ahead, we'd love to see you," whether it was true or not. And for me, she thought, it really is true, though she doubted it was for Boyd. Edward had a charming way of annoying Boyd, she thought, though Boyd wouldn't say charming.

Patricia stood out on the porch of the cottage (theirs for the summer) and looked out at the nearest mountain, thinking about Edward. Boyd soon joined her. "Wonder what he's got in mind."

"Oh, he won't be a bother. He'll probably be going on someplace else."

She could have asked, but didn't, just what it was Boyd thought

Edward had in mind. Money used to be a problem for him, but family business might also be involved. Boyd never cared for him; she knew Edward was acknowledging that.

"Maybe he just wants to see us," she offered.

"Why not a dozen other people?"

"Those, too. He has affections. And God knows after what's happened he needs to find some."

"Nobody on the West Coast has any?"

"Well, but his wife died. Outside of that—"

"You'll ask."

"Certainly I'll ask. He'll tell me."

"But then you won't know either."

She whirled around, annoyed. "Don't brand him as a liar before he even gets here." Boyd apologized. "He's your cousin," he allowed."

Patricia said what she always said, "But we're not close kin. In fact, hardly at all." Boyd had learned that just as there were complicated ways Mississippians took of proving kin, so there were also similar ways of disproving it. "God knows," he once remarked, "all of you down there seem to be kin." They dropped the subject of Edward.

Boyd spent the afternoon picking up fallen tree limbs from the slope back of the house. There were pinecones too. He built a fire every night, pleased to be in the mountains in midsummer and need one. Boyd was from Raleigh, in flatter country, but he loved the Smokies. "My native land," he crooned to Patricia, "from the mountains to the sea." Patricia said she liked to look at them, but never ask her to climb one. She wasn't all that keen on driving in them either, though the next afternoon would find her whirling down the curves to Asheville. "I've got to go in anyway, to pick up groceries, oh, and mail off Mama's birthday present, else she won't get it in time."

"And pick up Edward," Boyd said.

"You won't mind," she said. "He'll be nice. I'll cook something good, you'll see."

But she had hardly made it out to the car when she heard the hornet buzz of a motorcycle coming up the Asheville road. It banked to pull in their drive and under the helmet and goggles she recognized her son. Oh Lord, thought Patricia. Why now? Then she was running forward to embrace him and hear about why now and calling to Boyd and finally getting into the car, leaving father and son to their backslapping and Whatderyaknows. A long weekend away from school. He might have told them. Boyd's shout of "Wonderful surprise!" followed her down the swirl of the mountain.

And all the way she wondered if the mystery could possibly come up again. They had been over it before and decided it was just a joke of nature, unfortunate, but only extended family to blame for their son looking so much like Edward.

◆

Airport.

The heat in Asheville had about wilted her. She entered air-conditioning with a sigh and headed for the ladies' room to repair her makeup and make sure she looked her pretty best.

But before she could get there, a voice said "Hey wait up, Tricia," and there he was when she turned, Edward himself, standing still and grinning at her.

He came forward and planted a sidewise kiss. But even those few feet of distance had let her notice that he didn't look so great. Older, and not very well kept up. Scruffy shoes, wilted jacket, tee shirt open. The blond hair was mingled with gray, but the smile, certainly, was just as she remembered.

He was carrying only a light satchel. "I checked the big one." He caught her arm. "We're heading somewhere right away and we're going to eat something edible. I nearly choked on dry pretzels."

She managed to find an ancient restaurant, still there from former days, dim and uncrowded, a rathskeller. She sat across from him, her questions still unasked.

Boyd was fine, she told him. Mark had just appeared. For a minute, she could plainly see, he didn't recall just who Mark was. Then he remembered. "Oh great!" he said. A silence. Food ordered. Time for confidence.

Yes, his wife had died. Yes, she said; she had heard and was sorry. He had taken up with Joclyn in Mexico, followed her out to Pasadena, knew all along she didn't have long to live. Why do it at all? Patricia had wondered then, now wondered again. Love, was what he said. It was reason enough. That was Edward.

"Oh, yes, Joclyn's gone," he said. "I tried but I simply couldn't stay on out there after losing her. I began to think Where else is there? I mapped out a plan. Friends in Texas, a covey of cousins in Chicago. Brother Marvin in Washington. You here. I picked you first. And then, possibly, back to Mississippi. It's always there. Maybe not the happiest of choices. But there is where Mama used to be. But she's gone, too, and so is the house."

"And Aline?" She had to be mentioned sometime.

"Oh, Lord," said Edward. "The eternal Aline. Don't ex-wives ever go away?"

"What do you mean? Die?"

"Or something."

"I always liked her," Patricia murmured.

"Spare me," said Edward.

Suddenly, Patricia felt terribly much older.

◆

Boyd was showing Mark around the cottage.

"Isn't it a good place?" he enthused. "It is owned by Jim Sloan at the office. They couldn't take it this summer. You can bunk in here. Pat will make up the bed and so forth. And the bathroom's here. But now come on out and look at the view. We can see the New River. And the nights . . . ! Breathe in the cool. How's the new course?"

"I need to talk to you. I may be changing majors."

Boyd groaned. "Not again. Well, we'll discuss it. Meantime, do you remember Edward Glenn?"

Mark, thin but sturdy, often called handsome, given to pleasing smiles, looked puzzled. "Cousin of Mother's?" he finally said. "Didn't she—?"

"Didn't she what?"

"I don't know, Dad. I just thought I remembered something."

"You better disremember it," Boyd grumbled. He was not given to subtlety but he felt he was in a situation where such was required. "He just called up and said he was coming. Uninvited. She went down to meet the plane."

Mark's young brow wrinkled. "I thought of what I remembered—or what I couldn't remember. Didn't Mama date him or something?"

Boyd whirled on him so sharply he startled him. "Do me a favor? When he comes, act like you never heard anything about him."

"If that's how you feel." He concentrated, then said: "But why?"

Boyd was irritable. "I'll tell you later. After he leaves. Promise. Okay?"

Outside in a flat side yard, Boyd explained he was trying to set up a fish pond. "Sort of kidney-shaped," he said. "Something to leave for the Sloans—they insisted on lending us the place. Just the utilities to pay, though I guess if the roof blew off . . ."

"But do they really want a fish pond?"

"No trouble in summer. Just stock it. Feed 'em. Winter comes, scoop out the fish, drain it, leave it. We can start it while you're here." Mark had a look he got when something sounded like work. But then he got on better with his father when they worked together. Quarrels came when they pulled in opposite ways. He knows that, too, thought Mark. That's why he'd brought this up. Mark knew he had to ease his father into his new plans. Boyd

went to a toolshed and produced two shovels. With a plastic mea-
suring cup, he dribbled lime to mark the outline. He stood looking
for a moment before he took up a shovel. A sudden thought. "Have
you eaten?"

"I'm okay," said Mark, and drove his shovel in the turf.

◆

In Asheville, Edward and Patricia sat in front of a large house that was
half burned down, surrounded by guard ropes, now well into recon-
struction, which was not at the moment proceeding. It was the remains
of My Old Kentucky Home, the house Thomas Wolfe had lived in and
wrote about. Though why Edward had to see it, she wasn't quite clear.

"It's for my soul," he explained. "Tricia! I've got to live again.
Every little bit helps."

She was wondering what little bit Thomas Wolfe had to offer.

"Didn't Wolfe have to put up with an awful family?" Edward
recalled. "I wonder how he stood it. We were luckier than that."

"Are we getting into family?" She was tentative.

"It's what we share," said Edward.

"Boyd's family . . ." she began again.

"What about them?"

"I've managed somehow. I even get on with his mother." She
switched subjects. "You met Joclyn in Mexico."

"Yes, and I knew even then she was dying by degrees. After
that she went back to Pasadena. I followed. Then there was chemo,
all sorts of cures. But through it all she was happy. We were happy."

"Was that your reward?"

"Um. The trouble now is, she was terribly rich. I didn't know how rich. It was some family legacy. Who's ever going to believe I didn't do it for that? Didn't even know a lot about it. Who'd believe it?"

"Nobody in Mississippi," she was quick to say.

Edward laughed. "Right on." A pause, then, "How did this house burn?"

"If I knew I've forgotten."

"I read Wolfe long ago. You learn something from other people's bad times."

"Like what?"

"How to get through your own."

"Edward?"

"Um."

"It's Mark. My son Mark."

"Of course. What about him?"

"Well . . . I better tell you." She laughed a little nervously. "He looks a lot like you."

"Poor kid . . . only . . . Well, now you've said it." He sat quietly, slowly digesting the implications. "I thought that was a dead issue . . . Want me to leave?" He was half-joking

She was silent.

"Tricia . . . what if he does? Nothing happened . . . We both know that. We've been all over it. I don't even think about it, haven't for ages." He stopped again, realizing he was getting off on the wrong tack. "Let the past go."

"Boyd might not be the friendliest in the world."

"Maybe we can charm him with a drink or so."

"Just play it straight and we'll be okay. He's such a nice guy. At this moment you need us . . . need me. You said so. Besides, nothing happened."

"Tricia, *nothing did happen*."

"Right."

"Think of all Wolfe's talent in that one house. Busting to get out. And it did."

She started the car and backed away. Old-fashioned and rambling, the house had still managed to assert itself. The long-ago meetings, quarrels, seductions and heartaches of that big, lumbering man's life, the family's torments, had all smoked up right out of the windows and porches to sit on the backseat of the car, leaning awkwardly over, speaking in their ears. So time to let it out and then move on. Patricia thought she would read his book again. *Look Homeward, Angel*. Wasn't that it?

◆

Later than it should have been, they pulled up to the cottage. Boyd and Mark were out on the terrace, drinking beer and admiring the view. But the stunning moment soon arrived, as Patricia and Edward appeared. All they did, naturally, was shake hands, then stood there, boy and newcomer, look-alikes, though not quite carbon copies. Patricia removed herself hastily to the kitchen to stash away groceries, while Boyd turned and looked out down the mountain. The talk was prefunctory—weather, national news. Edward to Mark: "So what are you into at the university?" Mark to Edward: "It was history, but I'm trying to switch. I came home to talk about it." Boyd, disgruntled: "He's switched once already. Not good to keep on switching." Mark: "Computer science is a must these days." Boyd: "History is a great base. You can always take up the computer stuff when you finish that." Mark: "That's postponing." Edward: "I shouldn't have asked." Silence.

Patricia appeared with drinks. Bourbon for Edward with a little splash of water. Scotch straight for Boyd. Another beer for Mark. She had changed and smelled fresh. She settled into a lounge chair with gin and tonic.

"We started the fish pond," said Boyd.

"You can see the New River," said Patricia.

"It wasn't so much that I didn't like history. Old Douglas was interesting about the Greeks."

"The Greeks are important," said Boyd. "Ask Edward."

"So I'm told," said Edward.

"You all always knew each other," said Mark. "Funny, but I don't even remember kids I knew growing up."

"Well, being kin . . ." Edward began. "It makes a difference."

"Always at Aunt Sadie's," Boyd said with a shading of contempt, but maybe he was only recognizing their nostalgia for those youthful days. Patricia doubted it. She was bound to remember that one last evening. And so was Boyd. And so was Edward. And so soon after getting married too. Which made it worse.

She had often replayed it. Scene by scene, like a rented movie, its sequence never varied.

Edward was drunk and turning in. Boyd was drunk and staying up. Patricia was drunk and had gone to bed.

A house party given at Aunt Sadie's for Patricia and Boyd, bride and groom. What a glorious afternoon it had been! They had spent it walking to familiar places on the big property: the garden swing out near the lily pond, the winding path down to the stables, now empty, the old tennis court. Aunt Sadie, widowed but content these past years, with two gardeners to help, kept it all up. She had Lolly, too, a wonderful cook. Late as usual, Edward had appeared. "Well, it's about time," Aunt Sadie scolded. "We'd about given you out. Where's Aline?" "Home with a headache." Edward's code response, everyone knew. He and Aline were famous for pitched battles. Aunt Sadie gave him a drink. The guests were trooping in. It had turned black and was about to rain. Thunder grumbled. They all crowded inside.

"We'll play games," somebody suggested, trying to ignore the weather threat, though the sky had turned purple and looked low enough to touch. They were setting up a table for bridge when the lightning flash crashed right into the room and the lights went out. "Too dark to see aces," Patricia said. Edward declared it was too dark to do anything but drink.

"We could all go to bed," said Boyd, provoking laughter to acknowledge his honeymoon state of mind. Aunt Sadie said no, they could eat, as everything was done. She began looking for candles.

By the time they sat down everybody had taken a drink too many. They alternated between silly remarks, some known only in the family, and gossip about absent relatives. Both subjects made Boyd cross. Patricia could sense this, but didn't see it was so important or why they should stop having fun. The family didn't get together that often. He could stand them this once.

Somebody (must have been Aunt Sadie's big son Harry) also sensed the unease. He said to Boyd, "You can see what a crazy family you've got into."

"Well," Patricia chimed in, just being funny, "you ought to see Boyd's family."

That remark didn't work the agreeable way Patricia had hoped, but by then it was pouring rain. She was never sure why Boyd was so angry. He put down his napkin and got up from the table. Everybody tried to look like maybe he was just going to the bathroom. They ate steadily on, as though nothing was wrong but the weather. Edward tried to get Aunt Sadie to make a fourth for bridge. Everybody had another drink, which they didn't need. No lights came on. Patricia finally groped up to bed with a flashlight thinking she would find Boyd, but nobody was there. He couldn't be out in the rain, she thought, undressing, but as soon as her head hit the pillow, she went out like a light. So when the body landed in bed, it hardly registered, if at all.

It seemed scarcely a minute later but must have been an hour or so that she started straight up wide awake with the lights blazing and Boyd in the middle of room, yelling, "What the hell you think you're doing!" And ohmigod, it was Edward saying "Huhuhuh," rubbing at his head and straightening up from where he was sprawled out next to her. Patricia had always maintained he was fully clothed, though why she had to maintain it was the real question.

"You'd have to see he hadn't even undressed," she kept saying to Boyd, as they drove away that very morning, hardly saying goodbye.

"Yes, all right," said Boyd, "but what was the bastard doing in my bed in the first place?"

"It was always his room when he came to Aunt Sadie." Patricia had said it so often she was about to shriek.

"We won't discuss it," said Boyd. And wouldn't. Period.

But slowly it dawned on her that the reason he shut her up was that he didn't care for any of them, especially Edward. *He wants to get rid of all of us!* Such was the thought that kept hanging around like a bad child or a smelly stray dog, no matter how many times she told it to go away.

◆

Now the thought had followed them all the way into the mountains. Patricia was so annoyed she actually considered leaving them before dinner, with nothing to eat. But staying, she had to face it that the only really difficult person was Boyd. Edward was grieving over his loss. Mark was worrying about changing majors. But Boyd was sinking into a mood of long ago. Yet when she came in with a smoking cassarole, everyone seemed amiable, even smiling. Talking college days.

"What's Pasadena like?" Boyd wanted to know.

"I thought it was pretty nice. People out west aren't made like us. You had to make efforts to know them. Then it might not even register. They don't get into the politeness routines. Of course, Joclyn had friends, family too."

"I wish I had known her," Patricia said.

"It's what I mean," Edward said, half to himself. "Out there, nobody would say a nice thing like that." He smiled at her. Their kinship came back.

"We stopped by the Wolfe house," Patricia said, leaping to a subject.

Boyd looked blank. "The what house?"

"Oh, you know, Boyd. The Old Kentucky Home. Thomas Wolfe's mamma kept a boardinghouse. It's in Asheville."

"Of course, I know that. Insured with the firm. When it caught fire, we had a struggle over payments."

"Did somebody set it?"

"The facts kept dodging us. It could have been some sort of family jealousy coming out that way."

Mark said brightly, "If you get mad in a family, it just goes on and on. There's this boy at school can't see his daddy because—" He stopped.

"So what will you do next?" Patricia asked Edward.

"When my round of visits are over, you mean? I'll have to sit down and think about it."

Boyd regarded him as though he might be half-wit. For a grown man just not to know what to do next seemed hard to believe.

Edward said, "I'd move back home if it weren't for Aline."

"That's his first wife," Patricia told Mark. "He doesn't like her."

"She wouldn't be all over the state," Boyd said.

"Yes, she would," said Edward. "She's got a talent for it."

"Word gets around," Patricia laughed. "We never knew what to make of Aline. But we tried."

"I tried too," said Edward.

"Do you remember that evening when you had gone fishing and came in to Aline's dinner party with a string of catfish, when she had made up this important meeting you had to attend?" Starting that story made Patricia choke on laughter.

But Boyd was getting stiff. "All that family stuff . . ."

Patricia retreated. "I won't start it," she vowed. "I promise, cross my heart, hope to die."

Boyd laughed. He suddenly decided to be a good host. He went to work at it, asking if they had passed a highway project on the way from the airport. "Funny thing," he started out, and went into the funding, the business deal, the election that interrupted it, knocking out a campaign promise. He got them interested. His facts were certain to be correct. Boyd always said that to be funny you didn't have to exaggerate, just tell the truth. He said it was one thing Mississippi people knew very well. He said that now.

"Going to Mississippi is what I'd like to do," said Mark.

"It's not like it used to be," said Patricia. "All changed."

"Changed how?"

Boyd explained: "They don't have these big properties kept up by old ladies with lots of black help kowtowing and yesma'aming."

"Aunt Sadie was wonderful at it," Edward recalled, half to himself.

"She was getting dotty," said Boyd. "That's all I remember."

"She did her best," said Patricia fondly. "Right to the last."

"Was she my aunt, too?" Mark wondered.

"Great-aunt, I guess," Patricia allowed, then asked about football.

Mark was their only child. In spite of efforts, she had never conceived again.

◆

In the dark evening on the terrace they sat listening to a faint whispering of nighttime creatures, an occasional splash from the river.

"We could get the canoe out tomorrow," Mark said. "Is it still down there?"

"I haven't checked," said Boyd. "I'm sure they wouldn't have taken it to Europe."

"Maybe I'll go abroad," Edward mused.

"Ever been?" Patricia asked.

"Once with Joclyn. It was interesting, but we moved around too much. It might be nice just to find some place and sit in it."

"Wondering what to do next?" Boyd asked.

"Right," Edward agreed.

"Well," said Boyd, who was commencing to feel control, "you could go some place like Sweden. I always wanted to go there, but I never found the time."

"What would I do?"

"You said you would just like to sit," Boyd pointed out.

"The summers are too short."

"Try Mexico. That's summer all year round."

"I did try Mexico. It's where I met Joclyn."

"Oh."

Edward was silent. He seemed to have faded into the night shadows. He had declined dessert and coffee, wanted no more to drink. He came up out of his silence to say: "It was a pretty place."

Patricia knew he meant Aunt Sadie's place and she saw, as if it was actually there, the slope of the yard in the twilight and down beyond the drive the myrtle hedge and the fireflies.

"Lightning bugs," said Edward, echoing her own thought exactly. "Remember the time that——"

"I'm going to bed," said Boyd.

But when he left Mark wanted to know what time he meant.

"I bet he means the time about the pig," said Patricia, guessing. She was right.

"She made a pet of it and wanted it in the house," said Edward.

On they went, laughing and remembering, until Mark left for bed. Edward, finally rising, crossed to Patricia and kissed her on the forehead. She threw her arms up to him, and he was gone.

While still at morning coffee, Boyd and Patricia saw Mark outside with Edward, bending intently over Mark's motorcycle. Straightened upright and started, it gave a nasty cough and snarled. Mark shut off the motor while Edward speculated. He seemed to know what was wrong. Mark came in with a grease smear down one cheek. "We need to go down to the store. Can we take the car?"

"What do you want?" Boyd asked.

"It's something to clean the gas line. They'll know at the filling station. Edward says he can tell them."

"I had one in Pasadena," Edward explained.

Boyd gave his consent. The two got in the car and went away.

Patricia finished in the kitchen and came out to the terrace. Boyd joined her.

"They're gone," she said.

◆

Nobody had ever doubted that Boyd was right for Patricia. She had had a definite wild streak which she explained by saying nobody understood her. There had been escapades in the sorority at Ole Miss, sneaking out with that Osmond boy who wasn't the right kind, and then that wild night in the cemetery. Several had got expelled. It was said she escaped because of her good family. But then her own mother had run her out of church for showing up at Easter service in a low-cut silver dress with spangles. Yes, Boyd Stewart was the right one. For one thing he had a no-nonsense approach. He corrected her right before the whole family. "That won't do, Pat," and once he just said "Hush up!" The remarkable thing was she minded him. And after a year or so, remarked on in stages by home visits, she "settled down."

As for all the running around during those years that she and Edward had done—if nobody exactly minded, it was because they were kin, or near kin, thought of that way.

Boyd made money. He took life seriously. Insurance was a complicated business. He was still learning, he said. "But he must be fun, too," Aunt Sadie remarked. "How come?" her daughter Gladys asked. "Patricia wouldn't have had him if he wasn't fun."

They pondered over what the fun might be. They accepted

Boyd. When he visited, he unpacked and hung his clothes up carefully. Driving away with Patricia after that first visit, he had
remarked, "They're going to lose that place." "How come?" she
asked. He laughed and said in his brushing-off way, "They drink
too much." That wasn't what he meant, and a few years later, they
had to sell. By then Patricia was raising her baby and had settled
down even more.

Patricia and Boyd had lunch alone. Boyd wondered if he should
call the filling station. Patricia giggled. "Maybe they went back to
My Old Kentucky Home."

"Why do that?" Boyd asked.

"To look for Thomas Wolfe's ghost."

Boyd went out to work on the fish pond. At three o'clock he came
in. The sky had thickened darkly. He was sweaty; his shirt and trousers smeared with dirt. Patricia was checking the weather station on
t.v. He stood in the door and announced: "I do love you, Pat." He
sounded angry. "Why, honey," she said, "of course you do."

Something was happening, but where it was happening, they
didn't know. The first thunder rumbled.

Patricia came to Boyd. "And we both love Mark." Impulsively,
they hugged. There was a rush of rain and closer lightning. They
ran around closing windows and troubling about Mark and
Edward, who did not come.

◆

At twilight with the rain over and Boyd tired of ringing up with
queries, they heard the car enter the drive and leaped up to see.

It was Mark.

"Gosh we were worried," Boyd reproved.

"It was just raining. We thought you'd know. We had a couple of beers."

"Where is Edward?"

"Oh, he's gone. He said you'd understand."

Patricia felt the breath go out of her, permanently, it seemed. "Why?"

"He said just throw away the stuff in that little bag. He had a big one checked at the airport. He got a ride into Asheville. I offered to drive him but he said no."

"Well," said Boyd, "I guess that's that." Relief, unmistakably, was what he meant. "He gave me a great big hug," Mark said. "He said, 'Carry on!' Then he jumped in the car."

Patricia went inside.

◆

At dinner nobody talked but Mark and he talked his head off. He had been to drink beer with Edward! Edward was great to talk to! Mark could tell him things! He listened!

"About what?" Boyd asked.

"Everything. Girls and school and all. I could really talk to him. I'm sorry he went away."

Patricia got up to clear but Boyd said, "Don't worry, honey. I'll do all this. You go on out on the porch. It's cool out there. Look for the lightning bugs."

She sat in the dark and heard them quarreling. "If you think like that, son, just go on back to school and don't ever listen to me." They could say it was about school, but it was really about Edward.

There was no way possible she and Edward could have done anything at all that long-ago night, both drunk as coots. No, it wasn't possible.

Patricia got up from the porch and walked in the dark down to the New River. She kicked off her shoes, sat on the boat pier and put her feet in the cool, silky water. It was then she heard the Mississippi voices for the first time. She knew each one for who it was, though they had died years ago or hadn't been seen for ages. Sometimes they mentioned Edward and sometimes herself. They talked on and on about unimportant things and she knew them all, each one. She sat and listened, and let the water curl around her feet. She knew she would hear them always, from now on.

The Boy in the Tree

On a February afternoon, Wallace Harkins is driving out of town on a five-mile country road to see his mother. He was born and raised in the house where she lives, but the total impracticality of keeping an aging lady out there alone in that large a place is beginning to trouble him.

His mother does not know he is coming. He used to try to telephone, but sometimes she doesn't answer. She will never admit either to not hearing the ring, or to not being in the mood to pick up the receiver, though one or the other must be true.

At the moment Mrs. Harkins is polishing some silver at the kitchen sink. At times she looks out in the yard. In winter the pecan trees are gray and bare—a network of gray branches, the ones near the trunk large as a man's wrist, the smaller ones reaching out, lacing and dividing, all going toward cold outer air. Sometimes Mrs. Harkins sees a boy sitting halfway up a tree, among the branches. Who is he? Why is he there? Sometimes he isn't there.

She often looks out the back rather than the front. For one thing the kitchen is in the back of the house, so it's easy. But for another, there is expectation. Of what? That she doesn't know. Of someone? Of something? Strange mule, strange dog, strange man or woman? So far lately there has only been the boy. When her son Wallace appears out of nowhere (she hasn't heard the car), she tells him about it.

"Sure you're not seeing things?" he teases.

"I do see things," she tells him, "but the things I see are there."

He hopes she'll start seeing things that aren't there in order to talk her into a "retirement community."

"You mean a nursing home," she always says. "Call it what you mean."

"It isn't like that," he would counter.

"There isn't one here," she would object.

"Certainly there is. Just outside town. Two in fact, one out the other way."

"If I was there I wouldn't be here."

That was for sure. Once, over another matter, she had chased him out of the house waving the broom at him. She was laughing, to show she didn't really mean it, but then she dropped the broom and threw an old cracked teacup, which caught him back of the right ear and bled. "Oh, I'm so sorry, I'm so sorry," she said. And ran right up and kissed where it bled. But she was laughing still, the whole time. How did you know which she meant, the throwing or the kissing?

He dared to mention it to his wife Jenny when he got home. His mother and his wife had been at odds for so many years he believed they never thought of it anymore, but when he said, "Which did she mean?" his wife said immediately, "She doesn't know herself."

"You think she's gone around the bend?" he asked, and thought once again of the retirement home.

"I think she never was anywhere else," Jenny answered, solving nothing. She was cleaning off the cut and dabbing on antiseptic which stung.

His problem was women, he told himself. But going up to his office that morning, he almost had a wreck.

The occasion was the sight of a boy standing on a street corner. It was the division of crossing streets just after passing the main business street and just before the block containing the post office and bank. The boy was wearing knee britches, completely out of date now, but just what he himself used to wear to school. They buttoned at the knee, only he had always found the buttons a nuisance, the wool cloth scratchy, and had unbuttoned them as soon as he got out of sight of his mother. As if that was not enough, the boy was eating peanuts! So what? he thought, but he knew the answer very well.

He himself had stood right there, many the day, and shelled a handful of peanuts, raw from the country, dirt still sticking to their shells. He always threw the shells out in the street. At that very moment, he saw the boy throw the shells in the same way. Wallace almost ran into an oncoming car.

Once at the office, he was annoyed to find a litter of mail on his desk. Miss Carlton had not opened the envelopes and he was about to ring for her when she entered on her own, looking frazzled. "They all came back last night," she said. "I stayed up till two o'clock getting them something to eat and listening to all the stories. You'd think deer season was the only time worth living for."

"Kill anything?" he asked, more automatically than not. He'd never been the hunting-fishing type.

"Oh, sure. One ten-pointer."

Was that good or bad? He sat slitting envelopes and had no reaction, one way or the other. He had once owned a dog, but animals in general didn't mean a lot to him.

The peanuts had been brought to him in from the country almost every day by a little white-headed girl who sat right in front of him in study hall. Once he'd found her after school, waiting for a ride (they both had missed the bus), and they went in the empty gym and tried making up how you kissed. Had she missed the bus on purpose, knowing he'd be late from helping the principal clean up the chemistry lab? How did she ever get home? He never found out for it was not so long after that he had been taken sick.

They took him home from school with high fever. Several people put him to bed. It lasted a long time. His mother was always there. Whenever he woke up from a feverish sleep, there she'd be, right before him in her little rocking chair, reading or sewing. "Water," he would say, and she would give him some. "Orange juice," he said, and there it would be too.

He told his wife later, "I can't figure out how you can be sick and happy too. But I was. She was great to me."

"You like to be loved," his wife said, and gave him a hug.

"Doesn't everybody?"

"More or less."

When he went back to school the white-headed girl had left. Died or moved away? Now when he thought of her, he couldn't remember.

◆

Wallace Harkins was assured of being a contented man, by and large. When troubles came, even small ones looked bigger than they would to anyone with large ones. Yet he often puzzled over things and when he puzzled too long he would go out to see his mother and get more puzzled than ever. As for his state of bliss when he was sick as a boy and dependent on her devotion, he would wonder now if happiness always came in packages, wrapped up in time. Try to extend the time, and the package got stubborn. Not wanting to be opened, it just sat and remained the same. You couldn't get back in it because time had carried you on elsewhere.

It was the same with everything, wasn't it? There was that honeymoon time (though several years after they married, it had seemed like honeymoon) when he and Jenny got stranded in Jamaica because of a hurricane, no transport to the airport, no airport open. Great alarm at the resort hotel up the coast from Montego Bay, fears of being levelled and washed away. They ate by candlelight, and walked clinging to one another by a turbulent sea. "Let's just stay here," was Jenny's plea, and he had shared it. Oh Lord, he really did. But then it was over. When he thought of it, wind whistled around his ears, and out in the water a stricken boat bobbed desperately. They both had loved it and tried going back, but this time the food was dreary, the rates had gone up, and the sea was full of jellyfish.

◆

"Mother," he asked her, "why do people change?"

She was looking out the back window. "Change from what?"

He'd no answer.

"How is Edith?" she asked. Edith was his daughter.

"Edie is failing Agnes Scott," he said. "She isn't dumb, she just doesn't apply herself."

"Then take her out for a while. Start all over."

I'll do that, he thought. Time marched along. He had gray in his hair.

"Do you remember Amy Louise?" he asked, for the name of the white-haired girl had suddenly returned to him.

"That girl that came here and ate up a lot of candy once? It was when you were sick. I thought she'd never seen any candy before. Before she left, she had chocolate running out of her mouth."

"Did she have white hair?"

"No, just brown. You must mean somebody else."

He noted the street corner carefully when he drove home. Nobody was on it.

◆

Wallace had always loved his wife Jenny from afar. When they were in high school together she hadn't the time of day for him, and the biggest of life's surprises came when years later she consented to marry him. "She's just on the rebound," said an unkind friend, for, as they both knew, she had been dating an ex-football player from State College, while working in Atlanta. "Just the same," said Wallace, "she said she would."

Jenny liked any number of things—being back in the town, a nice place to live, furniture to her taste, cooking and going on trips. She was easy to please. She even liked him in bed. Surprise? It was true that his desires were many, but realizations few. He had put himself down as a possible failure. With Jenny, all changed. She didn't object when for a warm-up he fondled her toes. She said it was better than tickling her. Who had tickled her? He didn't ask.

Jenny was pretty, too. Shiny brown hair and clear smooth skin. He loved the bouncy way she walked and the things she laughed at. He told his mother that. She said that was good. But when he asked if she didn't agree, she didn't answer. But actually anybody in their right mind would have to agree, thought Wallace. He caught himself thinking that. Was his mother not in her right mind? A puzzle.

"She makes you feel guilty," Jenny pointed out. "If I were you, I'd quit going out there so much. She's happy the way she is. If you didn't come, she wouldn't care."

"Really?" said Wallace. The thought pierced him, but he decided to try it.

◆

About this time, Wallace had a strange dream. Like all his dreams, it had a literal source. Out in Galveston, Texas, a man had acquired a tiger cub, a playful little creature. It grew up. One summer day, responding to complaints from the neighbors, the animal control team found a great clumsy orange-colored beast chained in the backyard of an abandoned house. The chain was no more than three or four feet long and was fastened to an iron stake sunken in concrete. In fact, the only surface available to the animal was cement, the yard having been paved for parking. The sun was hot. The tiger at this stage resembled nothing so much as a rug not even the Salvation Army would take.

Reading about it, Jenny was riveted to the paper. "Where's the bastard took that cat in the first place?"

"They'll track him down."

"I hope they shoot him," she said.

"You don't mean the tiger?" Wallace teased her. She said she certainly didn't.

What do you do with a tiger?

The event made headlines locally because a preserve for large cats was located near their town. A popular talk show host agreed to the tiger's expenses for transportation, release, rehabilitation, psychiatric counseling, and nourishment.

"Good God," said Wallace, "they're going to have to slaughter a whole herd of cattle every weekend."

"Maybe it will like soybean hamburgers," said Jenny.

"Wonder if they ever found that guy."

"I've just been wondering if maybe the tiger ate him."

In his dream, some weeks later, Wallace looked out the back door window and saw the tiger, thoroughly cured and healthy, wandering around in the backyard. He went out to speak with it. He thought he was being courageous, as it might attack. At first it glanced up at him, gave a rumble of a growl, and wandered away, as though bored. "You bastard," said Wallace. "Don't you appreciate anything?" Then he woke up.

◆

The definitive quarrel between Jenny and Mrs. Harkins had taken place rather soon after Wallace's marriage. They were in the habit of going out to see the lady on Sunday afternoons and staying for what she called "a bite to eat." Sometimes she made up pancakes from Bisquick mix. Jenny was holding an electric hand beater and humming away on the batter when the machine slipped out of her hand and went leaping around first on the table, where it overturned the bowl with batter, then bounced off to the floor. Jenny shouted, "I can't find the fucking switch!" The beater went bounding around the room. She was trying to catch up with it, but found it hard to grab. Batter, meantime, soared around in splatters. Some of it hit the walls, some the ceiling, and some went in their faces and on their clothes. Mrs. Harkins jerked the plug out of its socket. Everything went still. Jenny licked batter off her mouth and grabbed a paper towel to mop Wallace's shirt. A blob had gone in Mrs. Harkins' hair. Jenny got laughing and couldn't stop. It seemed a weird accident. "I guess the shit hit the fan," she said.

Mrs. Harkins walked to the center of the room. "Anybody who uses your kind of language has got no right to be here."

"Mother!" said Wallace, turning white.

"Gosh," said Jenny, turning red. She walked out of the kitchen. There fell a silence Wallace thought would never end. He expected Jenny back, but then he heard the car pull out of the drive and speed away.

Mrs. Harkins set about cleaning pancake batter off everything in sight, and scrambled some eggs for their supper.

"I think you both ought to apologize," Wallace ventured, when his mother drove him home.

"You do?" said Mrs. Harkins, rather vaguely, as though unsure of what he was talking about.

"I never heard her say words like that before," Wallace vowed, though in truth Jenny did have a colorful vocabulary, restrained around Edith. In the long run, nobody apologized. But Jenny wouldn't go back with Wallace anymore. What she saw in her mother-in-law's announcement was that she (Jenny) was a lower-class woman, common, practically a redneck. "She didn't mean that," said Wallace. "You can't tell me," said Jenny. Furthermore, she thought the results were exactly what Mrs. Harkins wanted. She didn't want to see Jenny. She had been waiting all along for something to happen.

Within himself, Wallace lamented the rift. But he finally came to consider that Jenny might be right. He took to going alone to see about his mother. Gradually, this change of habit got to be the way things were. In routine lies contentment.

◆

After the tiger dream Wallace went back again. He didn't know why, but felt he had to.

She wasn't there. The house still quiet and empty, she had even remembered to lock the door. The car was gone. He scribbled a note asking her to call him and went away reluctantly. She could be anywhere.

Wallace returned home but heard nothing. He fretted.

"Well," said his mother the next day (she hadn't called). "It was just that boy up in the tree. I finally went out and hollered up to ask him who he was and what he wanted. Then he came down. He just said he liked being around this house, and he wanted me to notice him. He was scared to knock and ask. He rambles. He's one of those rambling kind. Always wandering around in the woods. I drove him home. The family is just ordinary, but he seems a better sort. Smart." She tapped her head significantly.

"I dreamed about a tiger," said Wallace.

"What was it doing?" his mother asked.

"Prowling around in the backyard. It's that one they brought here from Texas."

"Maybe it got out," she suggested.

If only I could stick to business, thought Wallace.

◆

That weekend Edith came home from Agnes Scott. She had flunked out of math courses, so could not fulfill her ambition to take a science major, a springboard into many fabulous careers, but had enrolled instead in communications. She had a boyfriend with her, a nice well-mannered intelligent boy named Phillip Barnes, who in about thirty minutes of his arrival had made up for Edie's inability to pass trigonometry. He knew how to listen to older people in an attentive way. He let it drop that his father ran a well-known horticultural company in Pennsylvania, but his mother being Southern had wanted him at Emory. He was working on his accent with

Edie's help, he claimed, and did imitations to make them laugh, which they gladly did. He was even handsome.

Wallace, feeling proud, suggested they all go out to see Grandmother. Edith exchanged glances with her mother. "She won't know whether we come or not. Anyway, the house is falling down."

"She remembers what she wants to," said Wallace.

"He's got an Oedipus complex," said Jenny.

They argued for a while about such a visit but in the end Wallace, Edith, and Phillip drove out on the excuse that the house, at least, was interesting, being old.

On return they announced that Mrs. Harkins had not said very much, she just sat and looked at them. "Not unusual," said Jenny.

Wallace sighed with relief. For, as a matter of fact, the little his mother had said had been way too much. She appraised the two for some time, sitting with them in the wide hallway, drafty in winter, but cool in spring and summer, and remarked that a bird had flown in there this morning and didn't want to leave. "I chased him out with the broom," she said. Wallace well remembered that broom and wondered if she had made it up about the bird. Mrs. Harkins closed her eyes and appeared to be either thinking things over or dozing. Phillip Barnes conversed nicely on with Wallace.

Mrs. Harkins suddenly woke up. "If you two want to get married," she said, "you are welcome to do it here."

They all three burst out laughing and Edith said, "Really, Grandmamma, we haven't got halfway to that yet."

"You might," said Mrs. Harkins, and closed her eyes again.

"It really is a fine old house," said Phillip, who appreciated the upper-class look of old Southern homes.

Going out to the car, Wallace whispered to Edith not to mention what his mother had said. "You know they don't get on," he said.

But Phillip unfortunately had not heard him. Once back home, he laughed about it. "Edie's going to come downstairs in a hoop skirt," he laughed. But seriously, to Wallace, he said: "Gosh, I do like your mother. She pretends not to be listening, but I bet she hears everything. And what a great old house that is. Thanks for taking us."

"What's this about a hoop skirt?" Jenny asked.

"Oh, nothing," said Edie.

But Phillip wouldn't stop. It seemed that Phillip didn't ever stop. "She said Edie could get married out there. Can't you just see her, carrying her little bouquet. Bet the lady's got it all planned."

◆

No sooner were Edie and Phillip on the road to Atlanta than Jenny threw a fit. "What does that old woman mean?" she demanded. "She's doing what she always does. She's taking over what belongs to me!"

"But honey," Wallace said, "we don't even know they're apt to get married."

"They're in love, aren't they? Anything can happen. And don't you honey me."

"But sweetheart, maybe Mother meant well. Maybe she saw an opportunity to get us all back together again."

"With her calling the shots. She's a meddlesome old bitch is what she is."

That was too much. Wallace had looked forward to an evening with Jenny, going over the whole visit a piece at a time, and afterwards having a loving time in bed. He wasn't to have anything of the sort tonight, he realized, and furthermore his mother was not a bitch.

"My mother is not a bitch," he said, and left the house.

How was he to know that Jenny had been mentally planning Edie's wedding herself? She had got as far as the bridesmaids' dresses, and was weighing black and white chiffon against a medley of various colors, not having got to what the mother-of-the-bride should appear in.

Wallace wandered. He drove around in the night. He thought of the tiger but it was too late to look for the animal preserve. He thought of his mother, but he dreaded her seeing what was wrong. He'd no one to admit things to.

He went to a movie and felt sorry for himself. On the way out he saw a head of white-blonde hair going toward the exit. He hastened but there was only an older woman in those tight slacks Jenny disliked, wearing too much lipstick. He did not ask if her name was Amy Louise.

◆

In spring Wallace threw himself madly into his work. He journeyed to Atlanta to an insurance salesmen's conference, he plied his skills among local homeowners, car owners, small business owners. He even circulated in a trailer park and came out with a hefty list of new policies. What is it that you can't insure? Practically nothing.

Then, to his surprise, the way opened up for Wallace to make a lot of money. He received a call from some leading businessmen who wanted to talk something over. A small parcel of wooded land his father had left him just beyond the highway turnoff to the town was the object of their inquiry. Why didn't he develop it? Well, Wallace explained, he'd never thought about it. The truth was, in addition, he connected the land with his father who had died when Wallace was eleven and whom he did not clearly remember. The little seventy-five or so acres was not pretty; it ran to irregular slopes and the scrappy growth of oaks and sycamore could scarcely be walked among for all the undergrowth. Still, Wallace paid the taxes every year, and thought of its very shaggy, natural appearance with a kind of affection, a leftover memory of his father, who had wanted him to have something of his very own. And he did go and walk around there, and though he came out scratched with briers, it made him feel good for some reason.

"Honey, we're going to be rich," Wallace said to Jenny.

"Why else you think I married you?" Jenny giggled, perking up.

Still what surprised him was his popularity. Prominent men squeezed his hand, they slapped his shoulder, they inquired after his mother, they recalled his father.

"Why do they like me?" he inquired of Jenny.

"Why not?" was Jenny's answer.

But he thought what it all had to do with business. And he was still puzzling besides over what had happened at the last business meeting. For they had succeeded with him; he was well along the road. Subdivision, surveys, sewage, drainage, electric power . . . But suddenly he had cried out:

"To hell with it! I don't want to!"

He sat frozen, wondering at himself, and looking about at the men in the room. They had kept on talking, never missing a syllable. On leaving, he had asked one of the oldest, "Did I say anything funny?" "Funny? Why no." "I mean, didn't I yell something out?" "Nothing I heard." So he'd only thought it?

Standing in the kitchen that night, Wallace came across the real question in his life. He scratched his head and thought about it. "You and Edie, do you love me?"

"You like to be loved," Jenny said, and patted his stomach (he was getting fat). She stroked his head (he was getting bald).

She had calmed down since her explosion, but they both still remembered it and did not speak of it.

◆

The trees were in full leaf when he next drove out to see Mrs. Harkins.

The front door was open but no one seemed to be downstairs. He stood in the hallway and wondered whether to call. From above he heard the murmur of voices, and so climbed up to see.

His mother was standing in one of the spare rooms. With her was a boy, maybe about fifteen. A couple of old leather suitcases lay open on the bed, the contents partially pulled out and scattered over the coverlet. She was holding up to the boy a checkered shirt which Wallace remembered well, a high school favorite.

"Isn't it funny? I never thought to give away all these clothes?" she said.

The boy was standing obediently before her. When she held up the shirt he drew the sleeve along one arm to check the length. He was a dark boy, nearly grown, with black hair topping a narrow intelligent face set with observant eyes. Truth was he did measure out a bit like Wallace at a young age, though Wallace had reddish brown hair and large coppery freckles. They stared at each other and thought of nothing to say.

"This is Martin Grimsley," said Mrs. Harkins. "Martin, this is my son Wallace."

"The boy in the tree?" Wallace asked.

"The same," said Mrs. Harkins, and held up a pair of trousers which buttoned at the knee. "Plus fours," she said. "Too hot for now, but maybe this winter."

She had made some chicken salad for lunch with an aspic, iced tea and biscuits and banana pudding. Wallace stayed to eat.

"Wallace saw the tiger," said Mrs. Harkins.

The boy brightened. "They keep him out near us with all them others."

"All those others," said Mrs. Harkins.

"I can hear 'em growling and coughing at night."

Wallace asked: "Did you stand on a corner uptown eating peanuts?"

"Not that I know of," responded Martin Grimsley.

They lingered there on the porch while the day waned.

Martin Grimsley talked. He talked on and on. He had been up Holders Creek to where it started. He had seen a nest of copperheads. Once he had seen a rattlesnake, but it had spots, so maybe it wasn't. He liked the swamps, but he especially liked the woods, different ones.

Inside the telephone rang. Nobody moved to answer it. They sat there listening to Martin Grimsley, until the lightning bugs began to wink, out beyond the drive.

"Someday we'll go and see," said Mrs. Harkins.

"See what?" said Wallace.

"The tiger," said the boy. "She means the tiger."

"Of course," said Mrs. Harkins.

They kept on talking about the countryside. Wallace wandered with them, listening. He watched the line of the woods where the property ended. There the girl with silver hair would appear, the tiger walking beside her.

He was happy and he did not see why not.

Sightings

Mason Everett, a man who lived mostly happily in his own mind, hadn't any idea why his daughter Tabitha had come to visit him. It's true they never saw much of each other. Maybe it was a shame. He was neutral on the subject. He had long loved her at a distance but now she was close she brought back shadows. Still he was willing to find out what she wanted. Her mother, in far-off Maryland, was maybe the one to ask. On the other hand her mother might be the very reason she headed his way. She arrived about twilight in a cab from the airport.

"But I would have met you," he protested.

"Too much trouble," she answered, and came right in with her duffel. She looked like all the rest of the ones her age, but also bore a resemblance both to him and to Celie. He remembered that when young he too had done unexpected things. She went upstairs to the spare room. She shut the door. Mason waited downstairs and thought about dinner.

Other ideas trundled through his head. Was she into a love affair, was she on drugs, did she drink, did she need money? If she needed money why did she take a taxi from the airport? Everything went in a circle until he heard her step on the stair coming down. She drifted around the living room. Did not turn on TV. "How is your mother?" he inquired. Tabby said her mother was okay. He had not counted on monosyllables. He tried several other directions, but finally gave up. "Is a steak all right?" She said yes. She also said, when asked, that she liked it medium.

During dinner he asked if she was in school. She replied that she had had to leave. "Had to leave?" he repeated, inviting her to explain. But she did not say anything more.

Mason wondered why he didn't push her further, but then of course he knew why. It was a habit formed long ago, not to go too deep, not to quarrel. If they quarreled they would get back to the accident, that blue blinding flash, that had brought guilt in, and blame, wordless until her mother got into it and a real quarrel started, the kind that spiraled downward till it reached a depth charge.

◆

He was walking his dog Jasper the next evening, when old Mrs. Simpson, who occupied her front porch as a regular thing, called out, "I hear your daughter's with you."

"Yes, ma'am," Mason answered, adding, "She can walk the dog."

She had walked Jasper twice now, once with Mason, once alone. He seemed content in his private way. Airedale mix, had looked forlorn in the shelter when Mason chose him out of others. But choosing didn't change him; he still looked forlorn. Tabby didn't pet him, but seemed to like him.

"What's her name?" asked Mrs. Simpson.

"Tabitha. We call her Tabby."

"Tabby and Jasper," said Mrs. Simpson.

Mason agreed that was it.

◆

In the years since Cecilia left, Mason had framed up his life in an adequate way. He missed her but not what she had turned into. But he liked a woman to be somewhere in his life, and when passing through one of the town malls he observed a likely one who owned a knitting and handwork shop. She was doing some sort of fancy stitching when he walked in. He introduced himself and found she knew him already. She had had some acquaintance with Celie. He said that Celie had moved away. Yes, they were separated. Too bad, she said, but things happened. Her name was Marsha. He asked if he could call her. She thought a minute and then laid aside a bright length of wool to write down her number. So it was easy as that. She had had two husbands, both long gone. He agreed that things did happen. Though he didn't see her often, he liked to know she was there.

Tabby began to catch the bus in the afternoon and to be absent until dark. He didn't ask where she went. But one afternoon he called Marsha, who didn't work on Thursdays. Mostly, he wanted to talk about Tabby.

"Can't you call her mother? Seems to me her mother should have called you."

"She did call. The evening Tabby arrived. I said, 'Yes, she's here. Yes, she's fine.' I hung up."

"You ought to have asked some questions."

"That's the very thing I don't want. I don't want Celie's side. I want Tabby to tell me what she wants to when she wants to tell it. None of this ought-to business."

Marsha laughed. "Well then you'll just keep rocking along for months and years." She sat in her big chair, doing handwork.

"It's fine with me," said Mason, and added, "She likes Jasper."

"Does Jasper like her?"

"He doesn't say."

"How old is Tabby?"

He counted back. "About sixteen, I think." He grinned, sheepish. "Actually, I'd have to look it up. I forget."

"I think you just better come right out and ask her what the problem is."

He didn't really want to. He remembered the terrible day she had blinded him, the flash of blue light in his face when he was trying to fix the electrical motor for her CD player. He was threading the wires together, holding them close to squint at when she had connected the plug to the outlet. His eye streamed water and blood and she yowled *I'm sorry* till her mother made her stop. It seemed to him every time he looked at her, she was yowling it yet, for his sight never entirely came back. Did it matter? He could read and work as he did before. The surgery had been delicate, one eye all but blind, the other intricately damaged. The accident gave him the chance to work at home instead of at the office. He wore glasses with thick hexagonal lenses and had to have special equipment to work with figures. Insurance supplied the major expense. So what did it matter in the long run? Sight-damaged people went successfully through life. It was well known. But he read it as a constant theme in his daughter's eyes whenever they met his, never to be erased. *I'm sorry, I'm sorry.* And instead of *It's okay, forget it,* his said now, *Why are you here?* No answers so far, but as Marsha told him, he had to try.

Tabitha had volunteered to cook dinner and turned out something done with hamburger meat that was edible. When he had praised her and eaten enough, she brought out some ice cream and he ate that too.

"Listen, honey," he started, "we've got to talk."

She looked up. He thought he heard *I'm sorry.*

"I haven't asked you yet. I was too glad to see you. But why did you come? Just to visit? No other reason?"

She played with her spoon. She let Jasper lick it clean. She leaned to pet him. "It's Mother," she said.

"Well, what about her?"

"She wants to marry somebody. I think he's terrible."

"Terrible or not, I can't stop her. What's his name?"

"Mr. Bowden." She winced on the word. "I told her, if he didn't leave, I would. She got mad. I think he's an alien."

"From where?"

"Outer-space alien."

"Oh." After a silence he said, "But if she's happy with him . . ."

"Nobody could be," said Tabby.

He sighed. He was a little bit jealous; unavoidable, he supposed.

"Have you heard from her?"

"I told her I was coming here. She was mad and shaking."

"She gets like that," he recalled, speaking half to himself.

◆

The next day Tabitha got a letter. Mason, who went for the post, saw it before she did. The lettering of the address was stiffly upright, like printing. He gave it to her to open and she read it aloud.

> *I know your mamma misses you, she says so all the time. I wish you would come back. We can all go out to restaurants and the movies. You wouldn't have to go unless you want to.*
>
> *Your friend,*
> *Guy Bowden*

"You see what he's like?" asked Tabby.

"Maybe he means it," said Mason.

"He's stupid," said Tabby.

They alternated cooking. Tabitha improved. Mason asked Marsha to dinner. Tabitha wore a bright blouse, brought up out of that bottomless duffel. She ironed her jeans and put on lipstick. She made a veal concoction, which was edible. Mason opened some wine.

"I'll teach you to sew," Marsha offered.

"Maybe I ought to learn," said Tabitha, and got dreamy.

"She's like you," Marsha told Mason. "She's pretty, though."

"Are you going to marry her?" Tabitha inquired later on.

"Nothing like that," Mason replied.

"What you mean, 'like that'? You sleep together, don't you?"

"Mainly we're just friends."

It was a week since she came. Jasper now slept in her room, lying near the doorsill. Sometimes he snored.

◆

There was bound to be a foray.

When the phone call came Mason was alone in the house and had no idea what to say. "I can't direct you here unless you tell me where you are." It was Celie, traveling with Guy Bowden. She thought they should all get together and talk. "We've got to understand things," she said. She had forgotten how to get to the house. The new highway had confused her sense of direction. They had stopped at a mini-mart to telephone. Mason knew where it was.

"Tabby's not here now," he floundered. "Get something to eat and call us back."

"We've eaten already," Celie wailed. She had taken on her desperate sound.

"Everett! Guy Bowden here." The voice was commanding. "We would like to see you."

Mason hung up. He wasn't going to be bossed around. Where was Tabby? Letting Celie know he'd no idea where she was—that would cause a flare-up. He shrugged into a jacket and took Jasper for a walk, hoping to think things over.

When he turned the corner to return home, he saw the strange car parked in front of the house, also Tabby, approaching from the bus stop. And now he freely saw what he had been thinking all along without knowing it: *It's her and me. It's WE. And they are*

THEM. Big question: *Did Tabby think so too?* In just one week it might have happened.

He hastened to her, heart beating with unexpected love that now came on full force, out in the open. How urgent it was. To love and to know.

"Honey," he said, "it's your mother."

"Oh God," said Tabby, and thrilled him.

He caught her hand. Jasper wagged to see her. They huddled, a party of three.

"I bet he's with her," said Tabby, adding, "Let's go somewhere else."

It seemed such a good idea that Mason almost thought it might work. But he was not entirely lawless yet, and they went in.

They were both in the living room. Celie looked as if she still belonged here and had just told Guy Bowden to sit down. That was the first thing. The next was how nice they both looked. Mason recognized that he and Tabby did not look nice. They looked scruffy.

Guy Bowden was a beefy fellow, large arms, thick legs, heavy feet. But wearing a nicely pressed gray suit, a satin tie. Celie was trim, she was a word he used to think about her: petite. It rhymed with neat. That was long ago when he was proud of her.

Guy Bowden was looking all around without approval, but when Mason and Tabitha entered, he at least stood up. Celie had rushed to Tabby, who now was getting her hug. Jasper growled.

"Leaving me!" Celie wailed. "It's been just awful, you leaving me!"

"Your mother's desperate," Guy Bowden said, and sat back down.

"How about some coffee?" Mason offered. "How about a drink?"

So was he being weak? It was what she accused him of, often in the past.

Tabitha got glasses and poured them out some Diet Coke.

"The lawn looks nice," said Celie, as though she had jurisdiction.

"I still have Aaron," Mason said.

"Don't feel up to it?" Guy inquired.

"Don't really like it," Mason admitted.

"Tabitha, we've come to take you home with us," Celie said firmly, and though it once may have worked, Mason saw it wasn't going to work now. She's grown up, he wanted to say, but didn't.

Tabby sat on a footstool with her arm over Jasper's neck. "Suppose I don't want to?" she said.

"Well, now," Guy pronounced, "there's been a legal agreement, as I understand it, and I think you have to, young lady." He spoke in a teasing way.

"I'm not going," said Tabitha.

They were silent.

Mason Everett regarded his ex-wife, judging that she hadn't changed all that much. He wondered to what degree he had changed. He wouldn't doubt he was showing his age. More wrinkles, a haircut overdue. Celie worked at exercises, she tried different diets, she measured her waist. She talked a blue streak about uninteresting things. She was talking now. There was a group she belonged to. They discussed single parents, problems with pre-school children, problems with school-age children, problems with adolescents. They called in experts and listened to lectures. There was this interesting woman from Canada . . .

"What do you do here?" Guy Bowden asked Tabitha, leaning forward. He sounded intently kind.

She took her time answering, then said, "I'm studying at the library. I'm going to go to college."

"Oh that's great!" said Celie. "I'm glad of that! But you can do that back home! I'll arrange it for you."

"I'm going to do it here," said Tabby.

It came to Mason that this was all a lie. He didn't know where she spent her time when she left the house, but it was the freedom sense he saw in her. He thought that was what she took with her wherever she went. It was what he wanted her to have.

Celie turned to Mason. "So you're doing that for her?" She seemed shocked.

"First I've heard of it," said Mason, "but if she wants it—sure."

"Taking things away from me," Celie said, and sprouted tears.

So they would be back into it, Mason thought, and saw the whole flawed fabric of human relations form, the present now becoming like the past, the future scrolling out ahead looking just as always, torn, stained, blemished. No change. He winced.

"How are your eyes?" asked Celie.

"Same as always." Silence.

For Guy Bowden, the moment had arrived. He leaned toward Tabby as if he were right in her face.

"Tabitha, you've got to understand that your mother and I just want the best for you, and what we think is that the best, the very best, is coming back to us. I know I upset you with some things I said. I'm just a rough fellow sometimes. But my heart's in the right place. If you only knew how I mean that. More than you could ever know. I mean it! I mean it! And where is my heart? It's right with you, honey. With you and your mother, she's just so fine."

Tabitha and Jasper both looked at him. Mason tried to look elsewhere.

"Don't you see, Mason?" Celie appealed.

"I think it's up to her," said Mason.

"Unfortunately, it is not up to her," Guy said. "I mean as I understand it, you two agreed——"

Tabitha jumped up and ran into the kitchen.

Guy Bowden rose with resolution and followed her, his heavy feet like a marching drum. They could hear his voice, muffled but persuading, "Now sweetheart, you just need to listen. And think . . . you need to think . . ."

Mason and Celie were left alone.

"Is he what you want?" he inquired.

"He's just so good to me," she explained.

Now was the moment to say, *So you think I wasn't good to you.* But he didn't. He'd had enough of that. What is separation, together or apart, but one long silence?

Two birds chirped outside the window. It did sound like a conversation, he thought, and wondered what they were saying. From the kitchen they heard something shrill, a sound as if it came from a stranger.

Tabitha ran. She shot through the hallway and was out the front door, running like a deer. Jasper was right after her, he made it through the door. Maybe he thought she was playing.

Mason jumped right in front of Guy Bowden, who was chasing her. "What do you think you're doing?"

"She's the one." Bowden was rubbing at his face. Had she hit him? "I was trying to be nice to her. Damn it all, I'm always trying to be nice to her. She won't let me."

Mason walked out the door. He looked up and down the street, but neither dog nor girl was in sight. She could have made it around the corner, or into the next yard. But which one? He called her once, "Tabby!" then decided not to call again. It was exactly as if she'd caught the bus. He stood on the sidewalk, looking all around. Next Celie and Bowden would come to the door and start talking.

He walked deliberately away. From the door Celie called after him. "Mason! Where are you going?"

"I have to find her," he said, not looking back.

◆

He did look for her quite some time. No Tabby, no Jasper either. He telephoned Marsha. Marsha said that Tabby was there, but she hadn't seen Jasper.

Mason got the car and drove to find them. Tabby was in the kitchen eating cake. The three of them sat and thought things over. No Jasper.

"Aren't you allowed to have her with you at all?" Marsha asked in an experienced way, two divorces and a grown son somewhere.

"It was something I could have arranged. But they let me know a fixed arrangement meant I could only see her at allotted times."

"And you wouldn't?"

"At the time I wouldn't. I was tired of fighting. Celie—you see Celie can keep on fighting forever. Nothing stops her."

"Maybe they'll go away," said Tabitha.

"Maybe they'll stay and just keep the house," said Mason.

Mason's reading equipment was in his house, also his workload from the hospital. Mason's present project was research in genetic statistics as related to disease. Figures from the computer flowed under his crafted Dome magnifier, a glass balloon large as a grapefruit. Specially enlarged from his machines, they arrived sometimes in complex pairs, wavered and spread apart; at other times they approached, hesitated, then matched up and marched together. He checked results and tabulated conclusions.

When Tabitha called, Marsha had left her shop with the assistant. She had driven to her house where she found Tabitha, sitting on the steps. Marsha was a good-natured woman, tolerant of human mistakes.

She gave a drink to Mason and a Pepsi to Tabitha. Then she talked in a quiet sort of way, about a time when she had lived out west, married to her former husband. She got out some knitting. In and out, the long needles kept to a steady rhythm.

Yes, it was her second husband she remembered most. Brad. The first she had been too young to evaluate now or ever. The second she had loved deeply, but he had always wanted to travel. His business was mainly in investments for himself and other people. He could carry his office everywhere—a computer, a cell phone— set up every needed connection in fancy motels. This was West Coast life. They journeyed, up into the Northwest—Seattle, Portland, sometimes into Canada. Then he'd take a notion to go south.

Mason sat and watched his daughter with his fragile eyes. If he only had a vision device to see into her being, discern her aim and direction, for even at so young an age she must feel something of the sort.

"You didn't want to keep me," she suddenly accused.

"That was then," he replied. "This is now."

Marsha knitted on. She kept journeying on as well. In the south, Brad liked to go to San Diego and especially always took a day or so for Coronado. There was an old resort hotel out there near the beach. He would switch for once from motels just to stay there. The food was good. He never stayed anywhere there wasn't some special restaurant to explore.

"Didn't you ever go home?" Mason asked.

"Oh yes, the house. It was in L.A. It was nice enough, everything in order. He left it with one of his assistants, a boy who practically lived there. Very nice young man, but then he—" Another story.

It was growing late. The rhythm of the long needles was steady. Tabitha yawned.

Mason was not supposed to drive after dark. Impressions blurred. He sometimes thought he saw someone cross the road in front of him when no one was there. Wary of arriving, he drove slowly home.

"I bet she was going to tell how they went to Mexico next," Tabitha said.

"Probably."

Tabitha said she was out of money. He said he would give her some.

He dared then to ask, "Bowden. Did you hit him?"

"No, I bit him. He bent my arm back till it hurt. He did that before. That's how I got close enough. So I bit him."

"Why do you go uptown? What do you study?"

"I don't study. I made that up. I just hang out. I met a boy I liked, but he's gone away."

Mason remembered the day they removed bandages from his eyes. He remembered blinking. Though dimly, dimly yet, he could see. He had felt a burst of joy, like a bubble.

He turned into his own street and crept nearer. The visiting car was gone. The house was dark. A shape was waiting at the door.

Tabby gave a cry of delight: "It's Jasper! He's come home!"

"And so have you," said Mason, and was happier than he could say to hear no denial.

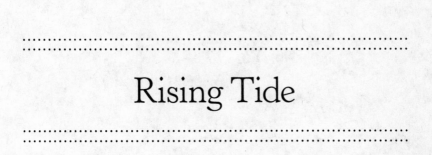

Rising Tide

*W*hen *Willard finally* left that day, Margery didn't even watch him walk away. If she had done, she thought, closing the door, she would see going away with him all those types he had worked with, whom they had met at dinners, at cocktail parties, at the club, at the golf course. And their wives, too. The ones who worked were interesting but tired; the ones who didn't work were silly. She had liked them all, or had said she did. Those bankers, insurance men, presidents of this and that, doctors . . . all that bunch who ran things. But now they were walking away with Willard. She wasn't sorry.

Margery went back into the kitchen and poured some orange juice.

She didn't doubt he would come back for something, though the custody argument had been settled, also the money questions. Divorce was wearying business but over at last, so why for the first time did she feel unsteady, a sort of wobbling on her feet now that her thoughts were at their steadiest? And when, in addition, she had just received assurance of the *job*.

Oh that job! Margery thought. It was going to channel her thoughts and efforts. Business composition, even if she couldn't get a freshman English slot, would lead to concentrating on something besides breaking up with Willard. She closed her eyes and put out a hand to touch something, something stable and reassuring. She opened them and was okay. She took up the letter of acceptance and read it again. A fresh start. She had said that to her daughter Elise: "I've got a fresh start!"

◆

Before she knew it, she was in it. She was entering a classroom full of waiting students, introducing herself, discussing, presenting, assigning papers. She came home weary but the weariness was a new kind.

A student named Sabra Blaine always sat in the same place, midway back on the third row. Margery Collins had judged him from the first to be from some Eastern country. Maybe he was from India, some obscure oddly named place, inland on that distant continent. He was older than college-age. He was small, slight, with a head all but bald, just a fringe of hair left to circle the back. He was always smiling. Smiling to encourage her, was the impression she got. No matter what she said there was the smile. When she said anything halfway funny, he nodded with enthusiasm. He got it, he understood.

Arranging for student conferences, she wondered especially when his would be.

As it happened, he signed up for the final one at four-thirty, at the end of the day. So in addition to going over his critique of an assigned essay, she walked out together with him after shelving books, collecting papers, and locking the office door behind her.

He had agreed with everything she said. "Yes, yes, too sketchy. Yes, not accurate. Yes, I should look up." There was the accent, singsong, as she knew there would be, though he had never spoken up in class.

As they passed down the hallway and waited for the elevator, she ventured to ask if he was a foreign student.

"Foreign? Oh, yes!" he smiled with enthusiasm, as though the fact itself was a treasure.

"From where?"

He spoke the town's obscure name—Champore was how it sounded. "But many years ago," he added.

"Many years ago that you left?"

"Yes, left." They were passing the grill. He turned off from the path toward the grill door. "Please." He touched her arm. "I offer coffee."

For a moment she hesitated. Wariness with students had to be observed, and recently divorced as she was, she constantly felt she was learning new rules. But he was hardly the type to concern her, she thought, and agreed.

Inside at a table, he assembled everything as though they were about to feast. Two coffees, milk in tiny containers, paper packets of sugar, spoons, napkins. The grill was all but empty. "Please," he kept saying, as he offered items to her. "Please."

Not until they both were stirring their cups did he start to speak. "My mother was movie star," he said.

She all but laughed. "Movie star? In Champore?"

"Zampour. Yes. By accident. She was beautiful. Just a girl. They came there with a company to make movie. The director saw her carrying up water from the river. The movie was all around the river—crocodiles, cows, children, muddy places, all that is everyday to Zampour. He asked about my mother. The next day he looked for her. He found her and asked her to come let him take her picture."

"Then . . . ?"

"Then he put her in movie. She was driving cows, two, down to drink from river. Also he fell in love with her."

"He married her?"

"Only for short time. To bring her to the States. Also so as to let her have me, as legitimate child. But citizen . . . American. Always he intended leaving her."

"That's a sad story," she murmured. "So you aren't a foreign student."

They were silent. He was sipping his coffee. His teeth, she noted, as she had before, were almost the color of coffee, as though he smoked a lot. Or didn't they chew betel nut—something she had heard.

"Sad story," he repeated finally, and smiled his usual smile, which she could not interpret. Its meaning kept expanding. Did he smile in acceptance that life was sad, or from some philosophic attitude? Had some religion led him into it? And why, if he had come here as a child, or even to hear him tell it, as an embryo, did he speak with such an accent?

As though he knew what she was thinking, he said, "My mother took sick after so few years here. She prepared everything before she died. She sent me back to India to live with grandparents. Grandparents took note of facts. I am American. So, they said, I can come to America."

Margery agreed.

"I must get education. Education is very necessary. Without it, no one would have job."

"It's true," she said.

"Now," he said, "you have husband, house, home? You have children?"

"I have a daughter in college. I'm divorced."

"That is sad story?" It was almost a question.

"I suppose so. At first I thought it was. Now, I think that maybe it's a—well maybe not happy—but a necessary story."

He waited.

But she told him no more and he began to smile.

Walking back to her car, she wondered at how quickly they had come to confiding. She had the feeling he was lonely. Had he no one here? No friends? Certainly no family, from what he said.

A week later she saw him on campus with a young girl taller than himself, wearing very short shorts and sandals. Her legs were long and thin. She was brown-skinned, and might possibly also be Indian, Margery thought. So he had found someone. But maybe she was a classmate, in some other class.

The day after this sighting, Sabra Blaine lingered after class and again accompanied her down the stairs.

"You will find someone soon," he told her. "You are blond."

What's blond got to do with it? she almost snapped, but did not.

His assumption that she was looking for someone irritated her. Dr. Marino, the psychologist she sometimes saw, listened carefully.

"You feel vulnerable since you left your husband," he said. "He may be wrong, but do you have a reason to think he was insulting?"

"I suppose not." Still she was dissatisfied.

◆

Afternoons, when Margery came home from the university, her daughter Elise was often there, either looking at TV or snacking out of the refrigerator. There was a thin line of small quarrels between them, something apt to go on indefinitely; it often vanished altogether, only to return. Elise wanted to have a year of study abroad. Her father favored this but could not afford it. He could, he promised, help her mother afford it. Her mother didn't want her to go. She had other uses for the money. And was Elise grown up enough to look after herself? Her tumbled dorm room, her disorganized study habits would tell you no, but changes often took place when other scenes and people took over. Perhaps she would manage all right, in company, of course, with other students. The matter was still unresolved and meantime Elise complained. Food was her special subject. She liked Chinese food. "I can't cook that," Margery had told her. "I can't begin to learn. Buy it frozen. Or we can send out for it." So they did, at least once a week. She usually returned to the dorm, but last night rain had blown in on her bed because she had left the window open. "I didn't notice," she said. "I didn't even hear it. I'll sleep here tonight. It has to dry."

"Does she miss her father?" Dr. Marino asked.

"She never says so. She can go spend weekends with him whenever she wants. Lately she hasn't mentioned him."

"Girls her age are often restless," the doctor said. Was he Spanish or Italian?

◆

When Sabra Blaine got into trouble he sent for Margery. She went down to the police station where he had been detained, to see about him. He had a cut on the side of his face which was still bleeding and his clothes looked dirty and scuffed, pulled about. They were about to take him up to the emergency room at the hospital to get him sewed up, but first it had to be told her that he had gotten into a brawl at a fraternity house.

"You are related?" the officer asked in some wonderment, as nobody could look less kin to Sabra Blaine than she.

"Not at all," she said.

"She is friend," Sabra said. When he smiled, more blood came out. He was holding a towel to his face.

"At the fraternity house? They should have called the campus police."

"It didn't stop there," said the officer. "They kept it up downtown."

"Who did this?" she asked. "He must know who it was."

"He doesn't know the name or doesn't like to tell us."

"I would tell you," said Sabra, "except that in fraternity they thought I was stealing something. If I tell who hit me, he will say what he thought and I will have to prove it not true. This I do not wish. Now we go to hospital?"

"Do you vouch for him?" the officer asked Margery.

"He's a good student, an A student. I teach business composition and reading comprehension."

It was Saturday. Margery waited in the hospital waiting room while Sabra Blaine got sewed up, endured penicillin and tetanus injections, and was bandaged. They went out together.

"I must get lawyer," said Sabra.

She started. "Why?"

"Things broken up. A very hard fight. In a way, I like. How good to strike. But now to pay for everything. Lawyer, estimates, repairs . . ."

What had started at the fraternity house, it turned out, was that Sabra was searching for Paula. Paula was the thin long-legged girl Margery had seen him with. She had gone to the fraternity house with a student older than she.

"You were jealous?"

"She is like sister, like little sister. I know she would find no good in that house. They hid her from me behind the curtain. But I knew. I seized curtain. It all came down. Crash on a table. Many things broken. She was there. I was right. 'Paula,' I said, 'you must leave now.' Then he struck me."

"Did she leave?"

"She did. I tell you, she is like sister. She knows when I speak like family speech."

"So what next?"

"This student followed me to town. He came out of alley. I was about to eat in a restaurant. Bar-B-Q. We fought. There was police and he ran. If I would say his name, they would find him. I do not wish to say."

"You mustn't get yourself in trouble now," she warned him. "Any more of this and the university—"

He raised his hand. "No more! I promise!" Then he laughed as if everything had been a joke, a sort of playing bad instead of being so.

"Sabra, don't you have any money?"

"Money?" He looked at her oddly, as if he didn't know what that was. He looked as if he might pay bills in elephant tusks and crocodile skins. "Come. I buy you coffee."

Instead she drove him home. Home was a dormitory room, the very end of an old building, just at the edge of a sharp slant in the terrain and looking as if it might slide off. "I have coffee," he offered. "Tea also."

Margery shook her head but inquired: "Sabra, why did you choose me to help you? You've got other teachers, don't you?"

He considered carefully. "You have face of understanding," he concluded. "That is good."

Maybe I have, she thought, driving away. *The face of understanding.*

Margery wondered why she had troubled about him. Then she grew busy with other matters and forgot.

◆

Sometimes she went to see her grandmother, old Mrs. Tenny, in her apartment at the retirement home. Mrs. Tenny, in her nineties, had outlived all her children. There were ways, Margery thought, that extreme age was helpful, even friendly. For example, Gran knew better but felt they were all of them present. Just where, she wasn't sure, but certainly around somewhere. She frequently mentioned them.

She sat in an adjustable reclining chair so as to watch TV without propping up. Margery sat near her and held her hand. Mrs. Tenny switched off the screen. "Lilla," she began, "didn't bring cakes this week." Margery's Aunt Lilla had been dead at least ten years. Yet cakes did appear at times. Someone remembered to be thoughtful. Mrs. Tenny had a large connection, some alive, some dead.

"I should have brought some," Margery said.

"Store cookies," said Mrs. Tenny, though without criticism. "Still, she sent that gardener." She nodded toward the window and at that moment a lawn mower began to purr.

Though it was only a small lawn in the complex of condos, Mrs. Tenny fretted over the grass and nagged the staff until she got plants put in. "Please, Margery. Go tell him to weed the impatiens," she said.

Margery went from the room to the side door, which opened on the little lawn. There right before her was indeed the lawn mower and driving it was Sabra Blaine. She cried out his name in astonishment. He looked up and stopped the motor.

"Oh, miss!" He always called her "miss," this being the way he thought a teacher had to be addressed.

"What are you doing here?"

"I cut lawn." Well, that was obvious. "Is job," he added.

"I can see that," Margery marveled.

"Much good to work outside," he continued. "Fresh air."

She asked him to weed the impatiens.

"I know him," she told her grandmother. "He's my student."

Mrs. Tenny was scarcely impressed. "Wonders never cease," she remarked, and went on to ask about Elise, her only great-granddaughter.

"Most of the time we get along," Margery said. "I think girls growing up are difficult, don't you?"

"You never were," Mrs. Tenny smiled, her little present for the day. "But Lilla told me Elise was going out with a black boy. Is she?"

Margery started. She knew that Elise dated at times but never pushed to inquire unless the boy turned up and she met him. She had once talked over the question with Dr. Marino. It was better to leave her alone unless she wanted to talk about something.

"Not that I know of," she said.

"Well it's not for me to order the world," said Mrs. Tenny. "Maybe he's from Haiti."

"If he exists at all," said Margery.

"He could be nice," Mrs. Tenny said comfortably. "The olden ways are gone." Opening a box, she found some cookies. "Lilla must have been here. I don't remember."

◆

When Margery returned home she heard talking from the kitchen. So it was Elise with a boyfriend. She was divided between pleasure that the girl would bring a boy home to meet her and a little wonder if maybe what somebody had mentioned to Gran might be true. She went on resolutely and called out her daughter's name, entering. The two looked up.

"Mother," said Elise, "this is Carlos."

Okay then, Mexican. What did she know about them? Margery wondered. But what, she also added to herself, do we know about anybody? Certainly her husband's year-old affair with a colleague's wife had caught her off guard. It was the colleague who had exploded. No patching up after that, as he had immediately filed for divorce. Would I have wanted to? she often wondered. She thought maybe not. Seeing Willard grow lazy and bored with life instead of the competent, able sort she had married turned her off for good. A year of trying to get along had fizzled.

"I'm learning Spanish," said Elise.

"She is good," said Carlos. *"Buena."*

"Then you can teach me," said Margery. "Are you staying for dinner?"

He consented. At table he went on to tell all about himself.

Carlos had lived in a house with a dirt floor until he was ten. Then his mother got a job with an American family, in the town where the father worked for a car company. They made parts for cars cheaper than they could make them in the States. Soon the family got Carlos's father a job in the company and that made money coming two ways and meant a better house.

Carlos seemed not to think what had happened to him was remarkable.

"You had luck," Elise said.

"Everyone likes my mother. She is so loving. Not only to me.

To everybody she is together with. Mexican people are not so loving. She is the different one. So"—he shrugged—"all life is changed."

"Because of your mother," Margery half inquired.

"It is strange, don't you think?"

"No," she said. "Not so strange. But I think the lady she worked for had something to do with your good luck."

"Oh, yes." For a moment he concentrated. "That lady was unhappy."

Elise and Margery were silent, waiting for him to explain. He ate for a time, pulling at his piece of chicken breast with his fork, pushing large hunks into his mouth. He had nice brown hands. The whole of him scarcely seemed anything but admirable. He noticed they were waiting.

"Her husband sent their children to school in the U.S. She wanted them there. There was an English school in Puebla, near to us. He wouldn't send them there. Soon I went to that school. I learned to speak. You can see. I was like adopted."

"Adopted by them?"

"Not really." He touched his breast. "In the heart."

"Do you see them?" Margery asked.

"No more. They got angry with my father. He got the workers together for more pay. He did not succeed. Then there was no more work, no profit. Everything broke down."

Margery had been to Mexico once with Willard. It was the summer before Elise was born. In fact, it was near Puebla, she now remembered, that she always believed she had conceived in a Best Western motel. She remembered the outlying roads, the poor shacks, children playing with live iguanas, holding them up to sight like baby dragons. Hoping to be thrown a few pesos or a U.S. quarter. The dry, rutted streets led eventually to a smooth modern highway and the motel sign. The air conditioner worked.

"But they were good to you," she burst out.

"Yes, very good," said Carlos, and continued eating. Then he suddenly, looking at Elise, offered a whole explanation in Spanish. Elise said, "Oh, I see."

She followed her mother into the kitchen as they cleared off plates. "What did he say?" Margery asked her.

"I couldn't make it out very clear, but I think he said his father was a drunk. He hated Americans. But Carlos doesn't."

"Well that's good," Margery said, thinking of a nice family trying to help out some poor people they liked. They wanted them to "get ahead in life." Maybe to some people that didn't mean anything. Maybe it was just a cause for resentment, then a cause for rebelling. It made her angry to think about it.

◆

Elise often changed boyfriends. When asked what happened to the one before the present one, she would say, "Oh, he's around."

"Didn't you like him?"

"Sure, I did. But not enough."

Enough for what? Margery worried, but thinking she knew already, she didn't ask.

◆

At the retirement home, Sabra Blaine no longer mowed the lawn. A black man now pushed the mower. "They come and go," her grandmother said. "The black ones are best. They seem to like doing it." Then she began to laugh. "Oh, Margery!" she exclaimed. "For some reason, I was thinking of the house party."

Margery knew what she meant. At the time it had been funny.

She was asleep down at the camp her sorority rented each year for a party. She was fuzzy from having had too much to drink the night before. Even knowing they weren't supposed to, they got liquor anyway, mixed up with some sort of punch, and drank and acted silly.

There were some boys coming later. A bunch were down by the lake. It was past twilight and getting dark when she fell asleep. She was startled awake with a black face leaning all the way across the bed, not an inch away from her own. She screamed. Not once but twice and maybe more. Then the boy got up and ripped the black mask off, an awful mask with thick red lips. He was laughing at her and of course she had to laugh too, though shaking still and almost in tears. "Jes call me Rastus," he said. She didn't even know him, though why that would have made any difference she couldn't say.

"Why on earth did you remember that?" she asked her grandmother. She had come home and told all about it. Her mother had sympathized ("The idea!" she said) but Gran had giggled.

"Just thought of it. I don't know why. I just lie here and think of things. You'd be surprised what things I think about."

Margery imagined that she would.

"For instance," she continued, "did I tell you that Willard came to see me?"

"What on earth for?" Margery asked.

"Well, he mainly just walked around and around, but he did tell me that you were dating a Chinaman and that Elise had got mixed up with some Indian."

"That's crazy. Just forget it. Promise."

"I promise."

◆

"Have other job now," said Sabra Blaine. "Waiting tables at Mandy's Restaurant. Is cooler."

She was talking with him in her office about a paper he had submitted in which he set forth an argument that disturbed her. He proposed that when going into a business arrangement that if promising something did not suit the one who promised it, a complete denial of having promised it at all was not only permissible but might be used to advantage, that was to say, purposely.

"You realize," said Margery, "that this is not good business procedure. It would quickly get you a bad name." She had avidly studied for this job in business writing——learning phrases, proper approaches, ethics.

Sabra nodded, smiling happily. "Must use carefully," he agreed. "Not too often."

"But I mean," said Margery, "it's wrong." He was silent. "Don't you think so?"

"Is useful," he murmured, almost to himself. "In business useful is good."

"Not if it's wrong!" She was aggrieved.

Carlos came to dinner again, bringing a large melon. Margery asked Elise later if she really liked him. "He's very sweet," Elise said.

That weekend, Willard showed up. He had called to inquire if he might come by. In the living room he walked around, talking. He had always been nervous and inclined to pace. "She tells me she has this Mexican guy," he threw out, as though Margery had caused something.

"Yes, I've met him," she said.

"What's he like? She even wants me to meet him."

"Well, wouldn't that be natural?"

"Getting parents involved. It sounds serious."

She sighed. She also had doubts. "I guess we have to be tolerant."

"I'd rather know who I'm being tolerant about. I mean to say that if we object she might take to defending him."

Margery well remembered that her family had disliked Willard and look what happened.

Willard went to the kitchen, opened the refrigerator and drew out a beer. He returned with it, guzzling from the can.

Willard was not a bad-looking man. He was rangy but well built. He walked with a careless stride and seemed always on the lookout. He suspected life.

"She's had a good many boyfriends," said Margery. "Maybe this one will go along with the others."

"Maybe I'll say I'm busy," said Willard. He found the garbage and tossed in the empty can. "I'll say I'm out of town. Will call when I get back. Maybe by that time she'll have somebody else. Or maybe I'll see him. What do you think?"

She started to add something about the good name Carlos had given to his mother, but Willard would find that laughable. *So he likes his mother,* he would say. *Well well . . .*

"I'm not holding off because of the boy," he continued. "He may be okay. It's only that pretty soon we'll have the whole family crowding around. I know the type. It's just as well not to monkey around with that sort. Talks about them, does he?"

"He likes his mother."

"So he likes his mother. Well, well . . . Are they hooking up? You know . . . is he laying her?"

"I wouldn't think so. She stays in the dorm when she's not here."

"You'd better steer off that bunch, Margie. Get shut of him." Now it was his Southern small-town voice, which she had once liked so much until she had actually listened to what it was saying.

Still, he was good at business, and maybe she didn't have to take his ideas seriously. As for other women in his life, didn't some wives "look the other way." He sometimes called up at night, late enough to apologize (though he didn't), wanting her opinion on something. Had she been hasty? She wondered, but didn't know.

◆

A week later she had a chance to meet the Mexican mother in person. A smiling polite overweight woman came up to her in the grocery store. Her face was round and pretty; her black hair was pulled straight back and fastened in a knot. She wore a loose cotton dress and sandals.

"So your daughter knows my son," she began.

Margery allowed that was so.

"My Carlos is first-class boy. You should know that."

"He's very polite," Margery admitted.

"They would make nice babies," the woman said.

"What an idea!" Margery exploded, and walked off.

◆

She stewed with anger the whole afternoon. What did she mean? Maybe that *if* they got married they *would* make nice babies? Or were they making nice babies *now*? Back to Dr. Marino? No, she wouldn't. She would talk to Elise.

She got nowhere.

"I haven't got time to make babies," Elise laughed. "I've got to graduate. I'm working real hard, Mom."

Margery agreed. "So don't get into real sex," she advised. Surely that was the right precaution.

"Oh come on," Elise said. "You know that Indian guy."

"Ridiculous," Margery said. "Where on earth did you get that?"

Elise giggled. "I think Carlos knows him. He talks about you."

◆

Willard stopped her in the parking lot at the grocery. "Is Elise serious?"

"About what?" Margery asked.

"She says you are dating some guy from India."

"Of course not," Margery said. "He's just a student."

"Oh," said Willard, and left.

◆

The Indian guy worked hard in her course, heeding her admonitions about his business morals, though she suspected he did so only on paper, to please her.

"I do not have to work restaurant or mow lawns," he told her. "I receive money from my father the movie director."

"How was that?"

"I write to him, a most pitiful letter. I say I defend girl much abused, which costs money."

"Was that true?"

"It might have been," Sabra Blaine said blandly.

So what business was it of hers, she thought, where he got his money or how? Still, she was annoyed.

◆

A week later, visiting with her grandmother, she came out with the latest. "Now they want to have a party!"

"Who wants to?"

"Carlos and Elise. They just want something like a cookout, but if it's still chilly, they think we can just fry up some burgers in the house."

"Oh well, why not let them? It won't kill you."

She finally agreed. Elise set the night. She made out a list of names, twelve in all, though it kept changing. Sabra was on it and Paula, Carlos of course, and other names which mostly sounded everyday American.

"They're bringing everything," Elise warbled. " I said I'd buy some drinks."

Exam time was winding down. It was a time for summer plans and parties before leaving. Time, thought Margery that evening, for the doorbell to start ringing and so it did.

If there was any word to describe how the young guests came in, it would be "discreetly." They were quiet and polite, meeting Margery in her creamy slacks and blouse, saying hi to Elise and Carlos. Sabra wore a little cap. His tall friend had on a skirt. All were ready to loosen up as minutes passed, so that by the time they had carried their sacks into the kitchen and set to work, there were giggles and chatter coming in waves at the time.

How they were organized! Did they do this all the time? Elise knew the whole routine, knives and forks, paper napkins, ice for Cokes, burger patties on the grill, buns and onions. A football-sized boy dumped salad in their biggest bowl. His tiny girlfriend poured on the dressing. A cry of "Mustard!" sounded like an operatic wail. In the living room, moving a chair, a pair of girls almost knocked down a row of blue vases, which teetered, but stabilized.

Margery held her breath over the vases, then thought it was better to keep completely out of the way. She fled into her study and closed the door. She tried to concentrate on grading. She smelled frying meat.

When the door burst open it was Sabra, carrying a plate of hamburger, potato chips, salad. "Must eat," he instructed, and went to fetch her a Coke.

She knew what Willard was probably thinking. *Of course, they'll all get drunk.*

Not true! she wanted to reply, and was right. Out in the house, it grew quiet. They were feeding and so was she. But then the hum rose again, increasing; now Elise came in, wild-eyed. "You've got to come! Mother, you've got to come and see!"

So what now? She stood on the outskirts of the swarming living room. Cheerleaders, they told her. Two were "real," they said, and four more knew how. It was going to be a pyramid. A little red-haired girl in chopped-off jeans stood bravely while two more each grabbed a leg and hoisted her to their shoulders. Three more lined up below, lifting the first three. Would the redhead bump the ceiling? Almost.

"Which were real?" Margery asked, but got no answer except from Elise who said, "Sabra knows one." Two were black, one white as milk. One, a limber black girl in the middle, had skin like polished jet. There were low chants that everybody knew, mounting, rising.

WIN WIN WIN!!! GO, HEELS, GO!!!
SCORE SCORE SCORE!!! DEE-FENCE, GET TOUGH!!!
GET TOUGH!!! DEE-FENCE!!!!

The redheaded girl lost balance. She swung side to side. Margery held her breath again. Broken bones were worse than broken vases. Shrieks all round. The red hair, tilting, was a flaming torch. Arms rose up to her, brown, black, and white. Hands caught her by the ankles and she steadied. Everyone clapped. A milk-chocolate-colored boy, off in the sidelines, sat calmly beating a little drum. Sabra Blaine squatted cross-legged in the corner, looking like a cross between Buddha and Mahatma Gandhi.

The pyramid came carefully to earth. Cheers. You'd think there really was a game being won. Margery was laughing at nothing, elated with everything. She felt excited and young.

How they did clean up! Washing, scrubbing, bagging scraps and trash. How they did thank her! Elise hugged her; so did Carlos. "It was great . . . it was great . . . !"

Margery had not gone to bed so happy in such a long time.

◆

The next day in her office at school, Willard called. Could they meet for coffee?

She was pleased, for she wanted to tell him about the party. They sat in a booth at the grill.

"No, Willard, nothing at all to drink. They were like cherubs. And such a mixture."

"I almost came," he surprised her by saying. "Elise told me."

"You could have," she returned. She felt a bit put out. It had been *her* good time.

"Was there a Mexican invasion?"

"Only one or two. No kin to Carlos," she added.

"What's that you got?" he asked.

"Latte."

"Funny they call it that."

"Why?"

"Just coffee and milk."

"It's Italian."

They sat silently. He stared at her. "So you brought it off?"

"I didn't do anything really. Elise did it all and the kids."

"Margie, I got the boundary fixed for you. They'd copied the survey wrong."

It was a tax error he meant.

"Thanks," she said. "It saves me going over there."

"You wouldn't have known how," he pointed out.

She was sure they would have helped her.

"Then there was the car insurance. I got the adjustment through."

"Well, it was your accident, not mine."

"We needed to change the car title."

"Things do get mixed up."

He sat silently for a time, then reached to take her hand. "Wonder why we did it."

"Why we split, you mean? I thought it had to do with Janice and Bob."

"They split."

"I know."

"That's all past." He went thinking on, holding her hand.

"Is there somebody else?" she asked cautiously.

He shook his head, but she knew him well enough, the way he dropped her hand, to guess that probably there was, so when he said "Of course not," she almost laughed. "Is she white?"

He must have been holding his car keys in his other hand, for he went white himself and banged the metal on the table, rising in a fury.

"See you around." He slammed the grill door behind him.

◆

Back in the office, Sabra Blaine eventually came in, asking for his grade. An A made him content, but he noted her latent tears.

"Is unhappiness?" he inquired.

It was a relief to tell about Willard. "I was just joking. I didn't mean it. He always takes things wrong." She thought of the flame-haired girl, tilting atop the pyramid, and the multicolored arms from white to jet black, reaching up. She burst out, "And what did it matter anyway?"

Sabra meditated. "Is difficult. Some seek many years for endings, but never find. But you—you succeed!" He beamed at her.

Sabra was thinking of leaving for India and starting a business. He would deal in beautiful Indian things—scarves, shawls, rugs, much else. "You will buy," he told her, and beamed her his blessings.

Endings, she thought with relief. *Sabra is right. I succeeded.* Perhaps she said it aloud, perhaps not. She felt he knew it anyway.

They went out together. She kept on walking with him without knowing why. The past was dissolving behind her.

"I offer tea," said Sabra.

The Everlasting Light

Kemp Donahue was standing at the window one December afternoon, watching his daughter Jessie come up the walk. Without reason or warning, his eyes filled with tears.

What on earth?

She came closer, books in her old frayed satchel, one sock slipped into the heel of her shoe, looking off and thinking and smiling a little. Kemp scrubbed the back of his hand across his eyes.

Why had he cried? Something to do with Jessie?

Jessie was not at all pretty (long face, uneven teeth, thin brown hair) and though Sheila, Kemp's trim and lovely-looking wife, never mentioned it, they both knew how she felt about it. But what did pretty mean?

Jessie, now in the kitchen rummaging in the fridge, was into everything at school. She sold tickets to raffles, she tried out for basketball. Once rejected for the team, she circulated announcements for the games, and lobbied for door prizes.

Kemp came to the kitchen door. "What's new, honey?"

"Oh, nothing. Choir practice."

Mentioning it, she turned and grinned, ear to ear. ("Smile," her mother admonished. "Don't grin.")

Jessie loved choir practice. Non-churchgoers, the parents had decided a few years back it would be in order to send Jessie to Sunday School a few times. To their surprise, she liked it. She went back and back. She colored pictures, she came home and told Bible stories, she loved King David, she loved Joshua, she loved Jesus, she loved Peter and Paul. Sheila and Kemp listened to some things they didn't even know. ("Good Lord," said Sheila, hearing about the walls of Jericho.)

"Choir practice," Kemp repeated.

Sheila was out for the evening at one of her meetings. She was a secretary at the history department at the university. Twilight was coming on. "Are you eating enough?" asked Kemp. He wanted to talk to his daughter, just him and her. What did he want to say? It was all in his throat, but he couldn't get it out. "Honey . . ." he began. Jessie looked up at him, munching a tuna sandwich in the side of one jaw. ("Don't chew like that," Sheila said.) "Honey . . ." Kemp said again. He did not go on.

After a lonely dinner at the cafeteria Kemp drove up to the church and wandered around. The churchyard was dark, but light was coming from the windows, and the sound of singing as well was coming out. It was very sweet and clear, the sound of young voices. At the church, there were two morning services. At the early, nine o'clock service, the young choir sang. At the 11:15 service, the grown-up choir took over, the best in town, so people said.

Kemp did not go in the church, but stood outside. He crept

closer to the church wall to listen. They were singing Christmas carols. He knew "Silent Night" and "Jingle Bells" and that silly one about Rudolph. But as for the others, they had a familiar ring, sure enough, and he found himself listening for Jessie's voice and thinking he heard it.

O little town of Bethlehem,
How still we see thee lie
Above thy deep and dreamless sleep
The silent stars go by;
Yet in thy dark streets shineth
The everlasting light . . .

"Everlasting light . . ." That stuck in Kemp's mind. He kept repeating it. He strained to hear the rest. What came after "little town," and "dreamless sleep" and "silent stars"? He was leaning against the wall, puzzling out the words until the song faded, and he could even hear the rap of the choir director's wand, and his voice too. Another song?

Kemp looked up. A strange woman was approaching the church and was looking at him. She was stooped over and white-haired and every bit of her said he'd no business leaning up against the church wall on a December night. He straightened, smiled and spoke to her and hastened away, pursued by strains of

Away in a manger,
No crib for his bed,
The little Lord Jesus . . .

At breakfast the next morning, Kemp said, "Tell me, Jessie, what's that Christmas carol that says something about 'the everlasting light' . . . ?"

Jessie told him. She knew the whole thing. She was about to start on "Joy to the World," but her mother stopped her. "Your eggs are getting cold as ice," she pointed out firmly.

"Why don't we all go to church tomorrow," Kemp proposed. "We can hear them all sing."

Sheila valued her Sunday sleep more than average, but she finally agreed and the Donahues, arriving in good time, listened to all sorts of prayers and Bible readings and music and a sermon too. Everyone was glad to see them. Jessie wore her little white robe.

"Well, now," said Kemp when they reached home, "maybe that's how Sunday ought to be."

Sheila looked at him in something like alarm.

❖

Sheila was from New England, graduate of one of those schools people spoke of with awe. Kemp was Virginia-born and though it seemed odd for a Southern family, he had never been encouraged to attend church. Kemp did audits for a Piedmont chain of stores selling auto parts; he drove a good bit to various locations. Driving alone, he found himself repeating, "dark streets . . . the everlasting light . . ." He especially liked that last. Didn't it just *sound* everlasting? Then, because they didn't have one, he had sneaked and borrowed Jessie's Bible. It took him a long time, but he found the story and relished the phrases: " . . . the glory of the Lord shone round about them . . ." *That's great!* thought Kemp.

One week more and it would be the weekend of Christmas. Sheila said at breakfast, "Now, Jessie, you're certainly going to the Christmas party at school?"

"I have to go to choir practice," said Jessie.

"No you do not," said Sheila. "It won't matter to miss one time. Miss Fagles rang up and said she especially wanted you. There's some skit you wrote for the class."

"They did that last year," said Jessie. "Anyway, I told Mr. Jameson I'd come."

"Then tell him you can't."

"I don't want to," said Jessie.

Sheila put down her napkin. She appealed to Kemp. "I am not going to have this," she said.

Kemp realized he was crucial, but he said it anyway. "Let her go where she wants to."

Sheila went upstairs in a fury. She had always wanted a pretty daughter who had lots of boyfriends begging for her time. "She's impossible," she had once muttered to Kemp.

Church on Christmas and Easter was what even the Donahues usually attended, and this year was no exception. The church was packed and fragrant with boughs of cedar. They heard carols and once more the stories of shepherds and angels read from the pulpit. They heard the choir and told Jessie later how proud they were of the way she sang. "But you couldn't hear me for everybody else," said Jessie.

It was at dinner a day or so later that she said: "The funniest thing happened the last night we practiced right before Christmas. This man came in the back of the church and sat down, way on the back row in the dark. We were singing carols. But then somebody noticed him and he was bent way over. He kept blowing his nose. Somebody said 'He's crying.' Mr. Jameson said maybe he ought to go and ask him to leave, because he was probably drunk, but then he said, 'Maybe he just feels that way.' I guess he was drunk, though, don't you?"

◆

Through years to come, Kemp would wonder if Jessie didn't know all the time that was her dad, sitting in the back, hearing about "the everlasting light," welling up with tears, for her, for Christmas, for Sheila, for everything beautiful. Someday I'll ask her, he thought. Someday when she's forty or more, with a wonderful job or a wonderful husband and wonderful children, I'll say, Didn't you know it was me? And she won't have to be told what I mean, she'll just say, Yes, sure I did.

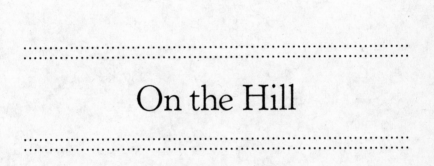

On the Hill

*R*egarding *Barry and* Jan Daugherty you first had to know that they lived out about two miles from town. Lots of people do live out in wooded areas here; the whole town is filled with trees so that the extent of it is not easily determined. Even so the Daughertys were to be thought of as distant. The little maps which accompanied their frequent invitations were faithfully followed, for they gave wonderful parties.

They had not been very long in Eltonville, only since last winter, it would seem. Exact dates of their arrival and acquisition of the property were not known. The fact was nobody could pin down any exact information about the Daughertys. Jan, in fact, sometimes went by another name—Fisher. But it was easy to think she was in the modern habit of retaining her maiden name, or was it the name of a former husband? The Daughertys, if asked, gave rather roundabout answers. Jan said, in regard to the name, "Oh, I keep it for Riley." Riley was her son. Then was there a Mr. Fisher, somewhere off in her past? It was hard not to sound too inquisitive. Riley was a blond little boy of about ten. When guests arrived, he ran about taking everybody's coats and then vanished with them, upstairs. He reappeared at departure time, looking sleepy but holding wraps by the armload.

As for the girl, younger, probably six, she clearly was Barry's daughter. But was she Jan's? Were there two divorces in the background? Not unusual: who cared? It wasn't really that anyone would care, one way or the other; it was just that nobody knew.

Going to the Daugherty house was like a progress to an estate. The road off the state highway wound through trees, but broke into the open on a final climb. The house itself sat free of all but a couple of flanking oaks. Its galleries suggested an outlook over vistas.

It was a joy to come there. How had they managed so soon to find such nice people? For a dinner invitation, you arrived just before dark and parked in an ample space. Barry himself would be just inside the door. He had a broad smile, skin that always looked lightly tanned. Sometimes a tie, sometimes not. He had picked up easily on local habits. His hair was dark brown, sprinkled with gray. He never slicked it down. And Jan? Well, she knew how to dress and how to greet. The feeling imparted was that everything was under control, and that the arriving guests were the choice people of the earth.

◆

It would soon be dark. Looking out toward the terrace from where she sat at the end of her table, pouring coffee while Barry refilled wineglasses, Jan would say, "Last winter during the snow, what a lot of creatures wandered in." "It happens in town, too," one guest would offer. "I admired them, as much as you can admire a 'possum—is that it? Those things with the long snouts and skinny tails. I'd hate to dream of one. I wonder if they bite."

"We'll ask Riley to find out at school," Barry said.

"They certainly bite," one of men volunteered, speaking from country knowledge. "But just if you corner them. They're sort of timid."

Where on earth were they from, not to know about 'possums?

"Then there was the raccoon," Jan continued. "What a precious little guy. All black circles under his eyes."

"You must have put food out."

"Oh, just a few scraps."

"They'll love you to death. They'll certainly bite you."

Somebody had a story about a raccoon his aunt had let in the house, because he looked so cute. He had rifled the cupboards and climbed on the shelves. He had tried to get in the refrigerator. How to get rid of him?

"They carry rabies," the same informing man said.

"Don't disillusion me," pled Jan.

Evenings there sped by, but when the guests spoke of them later, there was not much more to remember later than talk of possums and raccoons.

◆

Do we really like them? Eva Rooke asked herself that, all the while observing with fascination, as they were leaving the table for the living room, how Jan Daugherty wielded a silver candle snuffer, tapering in her slender hand, elongating her white arm where two bracelets circled.

Suppose I used a candle snuffer? Eva wondered. What would Dick say to that?

The Rookes lived nearby. It was easy to come there. Dick was with her sometimes. He could seldom be led out to parties. Eva gave excuses for him—as one of the county commissioners he often came in late and tired or had to go to some night meeting. But the true reason was his passion for music. He liked nothing better than turning up the stereo full force, four speakers blaring *Le Mariage de Figaro*, *The Barber of Seville*. Now and then something by Wagner or Massenet. He even listened to CDs of Broadway musicals—*Oklahoma!*, *South Pacific*. He wasn't choosy. Eva bought earplugs and swore she didn't mind. Once in the middle of gossip about local sexual affairs, how everybody wondered whose marriage would be next—she brought out that she was safe until Aida showed up. Someone who heard her caught on slow, trying to place the name.

Another truth was that people around Dick Rooke were a little timid. He was brusque with a habit of looking as if he had got himself bathed and dressed reluctantly. Everybody liked him, but found him hard to talk to. He said abrupt things. Something you had asked him five minutes before he would suddenly answer, having thought it over.

Eva, loving, knew she wouldn't be with anybody else but Dick. They had lost one child from a miscarriage but were hoping for another.

◆

Three times a week, Eva drove to her part-time job in a law office, about ten miles. There was a back road she took which led through some few unexpected places—a Chinese restaurant sat out on a graveled parking lot. A shabby old abandoned house with children's toys scattered on the porch. And a church with an odd name—Holy Brotherhood of Jesus. Eva always looked at the building, which was plain and small with a sort of square pedestal on the roof; it seemed to have been put there in expectation of a steeple. Soon they'll raise money for the steeple, Eva thought. But then one day, in the tail of her eyes, she saw the door of the church open and Barry Daugherty came out. A man in a black suit followed and stood talking. She swerved, almost ran off the road, considered going back, decided not to, and went on her way. Perhaps she was mistaken. He had looked accustomed there, and she was sure the more she thought of it that it had been Barry. He had a certain unique quality, not easily confused with another. But Barry in a Holy Brotherhood?

◆

That evening Eva told Dick about it. "Well, maybe he belongs to it," Dick said. The church was in his section of the county and he knew about it.

"What are they like?" Eva wanted to know.

"A bunch of kooks," said Dick, though he thought this same thing about most religions.

"How do you know?"

"Well . . ." he was slow to confess, "I stopped there to listen once. I sat in the back. They stand up and talk about it all."

"What all?"

"Oh, salvation . . . Jesus . . . stuff like that. They stomp on the floor."

"I cannot believe that Barry Dougherty is into that sort of thing. I expected they would join in with us, but they didn't."

"Us" was Episcopalian, the sort of religion that went with the wines and the candlelight.

Dick Rooke professed himself tired of all these dinner parties. Eva thought you had to pay people back. He helped out reluctantly when they did and Eva bit her nails, hoping things would go well. "You don't have to do all this," he would say, stacking wood to start a fire. She worked hard at it and was so exhausted afterwards she had to rest up for three days. But she loved those parties; everybody was so interesting. They were getting friendly with prominent people—the head of a university department, a member of the town council, a bank president. "You knew them all already," Dick objected. But it was the setting, the way the Daughertys did things. And the sense of mystery, the sense of belonging. Eva always thought they should have more of a social life. They had simply lucked up on the Daughertys. Dick had run into Barry in a line at the post office. They had got talking and the result was an invitation, the first.

◆

Barry Daugherty answered clearly enough when asked about his vocation. He was involved in a scientific project which might lead to breakthroughs in selected fields of cancer research. The basic work he had done at Hopkins had interested the leading research team here so they had enticed him to relocate. But where did you come from before that? Up around Philadelphia. What did you ask him next? Certainly he would answer, but what did anyone know about corrective laser surgery leading to alteration of enzyme deficiency? You switched to personal questions: Where did he meet Jan? Easy. "Skiing at Aspen. She fell and thought something was broken. Only a sprain." He laughed. "I picked her up."

So now, you knew everything you had asked. Could you possibly say, "What church do you go to?" Certainly, Eva's mother, active in the altar guild, could do that. But nowadays it seemed something you didn't ask, especially considering the Holy Brotherhood of Jesus.

She stood near a wall, looking at a three-panel picture, a natural wooded scene, each part a trifle different from the others. Barry noticed her. "It looks like Cézanne," she remarked, fishing up art knowledge from university days. "Exactly what I thought when I bought it," he praised her. In warming days, the guests spilled out on the back terrace. Once Eva was standing there, looking out toward a line of trees. She heard a distant thrashing sound. "What's that?" Barry asked. She shook her head. "You're from here," he teased her. "You should know. Have you got bears too?" It could be, she told him, recounting a story about a bear in somebody's backyard. Jan came out with another couple. "Don't scare me," she said, and remarked that Eva's dress was lovely. "You must tell me where you shop." If she hadn't come out, would Eva have asked Barry what church he went to? Not more about bears.

The time of year was leaning toward Christmas holidays. One day Eva went to the door and found little Riley Daugherty standing there in the cold.

"Riley!" she exclaimed. "What are you doing here?" She at once looked out to the drive expecting to see Jan in her gray Buick, having sent the boy with a message. But there wasn't any car or any Jan.

"Mamma's gone away," said Riley.

"Gone where?"

"I don't know. I'm scared." He was shaking, not altogether from cold.

"Come in," said Eva. "It's warm in here. Come on in," she repeated when he didn't move.

Eva gave him some hot cocoa and let him warm up.

"Why did you come to visit me?"

He looked at her steadily with large gray eyes. "Just 'cause I wanted to."

Eva had a feeling that was not wholly true. She told him she was about to call his mother. He only stared at her.

No one answered the call. *I'd better drive there,* thought Eva. "Come on," she said to Riley. "We'll go out to your house." He followed.

They were up the driveway and on the flat summit within shouting distance of the house, when Eva sensed that something was wrong. "I'm going to find your mamma," she said to Riley. "Now you just wait and we'll come back for you."

Riley said nothing. He continued to stare out the window.

She went toward the house with what she hoped looked like confidence, but the truth was, she was a little afraid. But why? She didn't really know.

She reached the door. The big bronze knocker with its lion head seemed to be meeting her eye. It crashed twice. She heard nothing from within. She circled to the right and looked in on the living room where the curtains were partially drawn. There sat Jan in a large armchair, facing a younger blond woman, who lolled in another chair. It was obvious, even without noting the glasses and half-empty whisky bottle on the low table between them, that they were both "out," as Dick called it. Stoned.

Eva went back to the car. "Your mother's not here," she told Riley. "Nobody's home. She must have sent you some message you didn't get. Now let's go have some ice cream, and I'll drive you back later."

"The car's here," said Riley. Had he trudged home from the school bus, then come to her? She didn't ask.

"I expect your dad came and now they're off in the other car. They'll both be back." I'm getting good at this, she thought. But dismay was growing within.

She did take him for ice cream; then, thinking Dick would be home and tell her what to do next, she rang her house. But what could she say? Talking on her cell in the ice cream shop she was in hearing distance of Riley. She clicked off before there could be an answer. "I need to stop by my house," she said to the boy. "Then we'll go to yours." So on they went.

"Isn't it fun to ride around like this?" Eva said. Riley said nothing.

◆

"If it was me, I'd stay out of mysteries," Dick advised her, having listened to all of it. He had gone with her to take Riley home once again. They had found Barry Daugherty out on the lawn. He thanked them profusely, saying that all that time he had just been upstairs taking a nap. Returning, Eva puzzled on.

"But you went in the church," she said. "You were curious too."

"That was before we met these folks. I wonder about weird religions. I had heard some complaints."

"But when they ring up again."

"For dinner, you mean? Just say no."

She sighed. She thought it was fun to go there. But she also wondered about Riley. Dick said she wondered too much. Wanting children herself, it was easy to let her mind drift toward the boy. What situation was he in? Who knew?

◆

Then Riley showed up again.

It was an afternoon in late February, barely tinged with spring. Riley, having rung the bell to good effect, stood before the door and looked up at her. "Now, Riley, what's the matter this time?"

"I thought maybe we could ride around," said Riley.

It was just as far to the Daughertys' house from the bus stop as it was to the Rookes'. She pointed that out to him. He said he knew that. "I like to ride," said Riley.

She took a long way around. A tribe of crows sped by them, turned and circled. They looked as if they were going somewhere on purpose. "What if you could fly?" Eva asked. "I wouldn't be a crow," said Riley. "Let's go away."

Eva was astounded. "Go away where?"

"Anywhere. Up in the mountains."

"That's a long way."

"Maybe the beach."

"Don't you want to go home?"

He thought it over. "Okay." So she took him there.

In the Daughertys' yard everything was quiet. The car stood there.

"Come on," said Eva. "We'll go in together."

She glanced at him. He sat very still and looked ahead.

"Don't you want to?"

Riley turned his head and pressed his face into the seat back.

Eva put out her hand to him, touched him to get his attention, saw he was crying.

"Why, Riley. What's the matter, honey?"

"He'll drown me."

"Who will? Your daddy?"

Riley suddenly jumped forward, opened the door, sprang out and ran to the house. He rushed in through the front door not looking back.

◆

That evening Dick was downright firm. "You leave those folks alone."

"I'm not sure if he even said that. I thought he did."

"There's trouble in that house. It's not our business."

But now she had office work to do and thought he was right and went about her daily life. But at times she wondered if Riley might appear again and there was a catch in her heart from that very wondering. Uptown she ran into Amy Waldron who said, "Those people quit inviting us, how about you?" Eva agreed. "I think her sister's been here," said Amy, "but even so—" Anyway, no more invitations. It seemed all that glow and elegance had just been phenomena of seasons past.

Despite herself, she would detour and drive past the Daughertys' just to glance at it as it stood on the rise among trees with the front drive opening and disappearing. All was silent, and nobody seemed at home, though sometimes a car could be seen, high up.

◆

Next, the truant officer. The son of some people she knew had been reported as not in school, they said, but the school couldn't find out why. They had visited but no one was at home and so had reported the absence. "I understood you all were friends. I couldn't find anybody."

"If I go there and ring, they might let me in. They have a girl too, I think."

The officer thought it over. "Try, then. But let us know."

Dick was out. She dressed carefully and then drove there. Why did her heart beat so fast when she rang the bell?

Footsteps, then the door and there stood Jan Daugherty in an old dressing gown that could only be called a wrapper. She looked drained, tired, maybe hungover. "Oh, it's you."

"Why, Jan, I just stopped by to say hello. I was wondering about Riley. Someone told me he hadn't been in school."

"He's sick. I'm keeping him in for a while." Behind her the little girl was lingering palely at the foot of the stair.

"Nothing serious, I hope?"

She stepped back, half closing the door between them. "Same thing his father had. Sorry, but I need to see about . . ."

See about what, she never said. Only "Thanks for coming," and the closed door.

◆

"Well then a mystery," was all Dick would say. She had called the truant officer. He had thanked her.

"His real father must have died of something or other," she speculated.

"Will you stop all this? I never liked them anyway. Too slick and smooth. Something's bound to be wrong."

"It's that church," she pondered.

"Not our problem," Dick said, and put on Wagner.

Seeing no more of them then, she agreed, was the only right way. Still she thought of Riley. There was something about a needful child, but what did he need? She remembered the large gray eyes, asking for something. One day, well and hearty, he appeared again. She drove him home once more. He told her he wanted to go see his grandmother. He said that she lived in Hollowell, a town some miles away.

"I can't take you," said Eva. "Ask your mom and dad."

"They don't like her."

This time, she dropped him in his driveway and left.

Long after the Daughertys had moved away, Eva found a list of Hollowell citizens but none of their name, nor Fisher either.

◆

It was only a year they had been there. The house sat empty for a good while. It looked lonely. Eva was happily pregnant again. Hoping this time to succeed, she quit her job. Dick had persuaded her. In the afternoons she walked, sometimes by the Daugherty house. One afternoon in the woods across from the entrance, she saw a small boy who beckoned to her. She followed but he disappeared into the woods. She stood a few steps into the trees and called out, "Riley?" *He's looking for me.*

Oh but that was absurd, she realized. The family had long gone and now the For Sale sign was down, someone else would move in.

◆

It was inevitable she would go to that church. She found out the time—it was the normal Sunday eleven o'clock hour. To Dick, at home with a pile of Sunday papers, she had only said she was going to church.

She parked near some other cars and sat quietly, listening. The church windows were open to the warm day. The people who entered did not look her way. They mostly wore dark clothes, even black. She saw no one she knew. She heard murmuring that died away and a piano began to play a tune she'd never heard. Singing too, then silence. The speaking voice—a minister?—was too low to make out the words, but before long it began to rise, even to shouting, and she heard "Water? Fire? Blood?" There began a sort of chanting and a shuffling like feet moving and then a positive shout: "We consume or we will be consumed!"

Good Lord, Eva thought. She slid from the car and moved nearer to the open door. She wanted to peer inside. A man in black stood in front of the audience, waving something like a pitcher full of liquid. A line of children kneeled before him. On the table beside him, a large torch-like candle was alight. The feet began to move again, the rhythm mounting, almost stamping the floor.

The door closed in her face. A man was standing beside her.

"What are you doing?" he demanded.

"I was passing by," she stammered. "I wanted to hear."

"Come in if you wish," he said sternly. "We celebrate God's power. You can join us. But do not spy."

"Those children," she said. "What is happening?"

"They are souls before God," he all but intoned. From within she heard a child's frightened cry. She turned and hastened back to her car.

It was telling Dick about it when she got home that relieved her.

"Jesus," he said. "I told you to stay away."

"But you went there yourself."

"I didn't see them trying to kill anybody."

"But you had heard things. You investigated."

"Yes, I had heard things. People complained. But what are you going to do about it? The Baptists keep a lake for dunking people. Some people wash feet. Up in the mountains, they play around with snakes."

"It ought to be stopped," she insisted. "What did they mean by fire or by blood?"

"People just like to go crazy. Religion's the best way. 'Do it my way, you'll be saved.'"

"Barry Daugherty had a scar on his face."

"Maybe they branded him."

They both began to laugh. She felt it had been a bad dream.

After lunch he lay down beside her. "What cold little hands." He fondled one. "Let me warm them for you." One of those operas, she forgot which. He sang it in the foreign words. *"Se la lasci riscaldar."* She felt a thrill. His hands were warm. For the first time, the baby stirred in her womb.

◆

"You ought to go to your own church," her mother advised. She was a model in attending. "We could get all that out of you. Anyway, what do you care what they do?"

"It was the boy. He was frightened. And then the crying I heard . . ."

The next Sunday she did go to church. She sat by her mother and listened though did not remember later what was said, but came out feeling calm.

So now the past had dissolved everything about the Daughertys. They had vanished like a road.

◆

Still, when she passed by, she looked up at the house. Then that habit too faded. She kept her appointments, doing everything as she was told, making ready for the child.

But one day, driving past on an errand, she saw at the top of the hill above the trees the high yellow lift of a crane. What on earth? She parked by the roadside and began to walk slowly up the drive. The crane was in the backyard of the house, which seemed to be vacant. There were two men in the back around the crane. They looked up at her. Another man was sitting on the small back terrace where Jan Daugherty, in warm weather, had liked to serve cocktails. She could almost hear the laughter. The man rose and came to her.

"You want something?"

"Why no . . . I was just curious, that's all."

He looked puzzled. She felt awkward, so obviously pregnant, so intrusive on the scene.

"I—I used to know the people who lived here."

"Well, they moved away. I bought the house." She still stood there. "It's mine," he added, as if she hadn't heard.

"Not the last ones," she said. "The ones before that. The Daughertys. They had children, I remember."

He laughed. "Don't ask me." He nodded at the crane. "Drainage problems. We've got to uproot the pipes. Hey, you walked here? I can drive you home."

"No, I'm okay." Coming closer to the house, she peered through a window, seeing the shadowy, empty space inside, as if she hadn't believed it could be. She could glimpse the living room, even see the entrance hall if she craned. Inside, she thought something moved.

"You look here—" The voice had turned harsh. He meant business. She hastened away past the house, down the drive. At a turn a deer came out from the trees and stood still, regarding her for a long moment. *I'm an intruder,* she thought. The deer turned and leaped back into the wood.

Before anybody lived here, before there was even a house, the deer were here. The place was theirs. She recalled the talk about 'possums and coons. The bear they might have heard. Didn't someone mention snakes? Animal life started spinning through her mind, all but clouding her vision. She sat in the car, waiting for it to clear. Inside her, the baby was stirring.

At dinner that night she told Dick, "I saw a deer."

"They're everywhere, especially at night."

On the way to the hospital where he had to rush her that night, they saw no deer at all. By dawn there was another child in the world, a boy. Her mother came to stay with them. She sat and rocked and changed the diapers and Dick was nice to her.

"I prayed she would be all right," she told him. "I asked for prayers at church." She was a comfortable woman, wearing old-fashioned shoes that laced.

Dick had arranged for a nurse who now sat there too. There was a changing table, a bassinet. "I always pray," the nurse said, and added, "I'm a Methodist."

At the hospital Dick had run into one of the doctors he knew from an illness in his family. Oncology. "There was a guy here doing computer research in cancer. Daugherty. He left last year." "They come and go," said the doctor. "Can't say I remember him." He bent to a computer and found a few leads. "Seems it fell through," was all he could report. "But I do remember now. Something about a child that died."

Eva dozed and woke. She put out her arms and the nurse lifted the baby to lie in them. Bliss was crowding into her confusion and remembered pain. "What's all this about Riley?" the nurse asked.

Her mother said, "She wants to name him that."

Dick thought, looking in on the scene, *three women and a baby son*. He heard what they were saying. "His name's Richard," he clearly pronounced. "We'll call him Rick." *I'll teach him music*, he comfortably thought. He sat down on the bed and stroked his child's head. He took his wife's hand.

"What's gone is gone," he said. "What's real remains."

◆

So they built the wall. From back of it, came the faint echo of stamping feet, and on the hill a bear explored, a deer was watchful, and a little boy wandered, searching forever

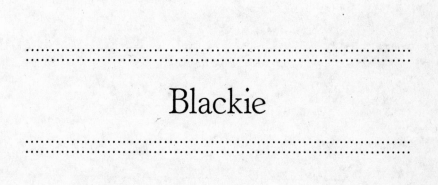

Blackie

1.

Able to stop work for a moment, Emily leaned from the upstairs window and looked out into the front yard.

Given this time of the afternoon in good weather, you could be sure that Mr. Earl was out throwing the ball for the dog. He sat in his adjustable lawn chair. All his chairs for some years had been engineered to support his various weaknesses of spine and leg, but his arm was still able to make good throws. The dog's name was Blackie, mostly Labrador, except for her shaggy tail. The goal of the throw was a line of hedge straight across an ample lawn. A good throw placed the ball to roll into the hedge, though not so far as to go through it. Weeds had grown up just beyond, on the other side, which was out of their control, and certainly untidy. When Blackie got too far beyond the hedge, she might come back with any manner of thing in place of the ball. Once it was a dead bird, once a scarf somebody must have dropped, yet again a delapidated straw hat, and another time a half-eaten piece of fried chicken. She carried all items tenderly, as she had been trained to do, placing them at Mr. Earl's feet, wagging tentatively while she awaited praise. After head pats she would return if need be for the ball. Then wait for another round. She was happy.

"Hup!" said Mr. Earl, and threw. Blackie bounded off.

"Daddy's getting tired," said Emily, and turned back from the window.

"Oh, let him play," said Hubert, Mr. Earl's oldest grandson, home from college. He was lounging on the sofa, clipping his nails.

"Come let's talk." Emily gestured to a chair. "I've not heard any news yet."

"Not much to tell." Hubert was often vague. He launched conversations when he felt like it, with his grandfather or his father, maybe with her.

Emily had three boys and Mr. Earl not actually to see to, but to be on hand for. Not very popular when she was growing up, she used to long for more male company while watching a pretty sister go out with one date after another. Yet here she was with too many males, including a husband whose business often took him away.

"Wilmer Lee!" she called out, hoping the middle boy was around to hear. She needed him to go to the grocery, though where he might be now was a mystery. When no answer came, she would call the youngest, Milton, who was always reading. He did not like to put down his book, but he would. She smiled when he showed up in the door. With affection you forgot annoyance. "Can you go to the grocery?" He would have to walk or take the bus.

"Hup!" said Mr. Earl, from the yard. It was growing late.

"What you need?" asked Milton.

From out her apron pocket, she handed him a list.

Emily had once been a woman with weighty responsibilities.

She was secretary to the head of supplies at the giant hospital in that city, and as such had been caught up in a scandal no one could explain or stop, once it got going. She was still trying to explain it to herself. It was her superior Dr. Ferguson's fault, but just how she could never say, and so at long last, after innumerable inquiries, she had submitted her resignation. *I shouldn't have given up,* her mind muttered away at times, and probably always would. But resentments did not push a day forward. Milton going for the groceries did that.

"You just said dessert. What dessert?"

"Anything you want. A frozen key lime pie. Ask Wilmer Lee."

Milton thought about it. "Where is he?"

"I don't know. Just think of what you want. Get that."

No one these days had much of an idea where Wilmer Lee was. He was careless and handsome, and gave the idea that he was into things he shouldn't be into. Their neighborhood was a mile removed from the town center and it was town that pulled him away. He had twice been detained for underage drinking and had had to prove his age. He had also been reprimanded for rowdy conduct. There might be another scandal, Emily thought. When she reproached him he had laughed and mocked her. It was hard not to laugh with him, but that would mean it wasn't important. She supposed it wasn't. When her husband Lawrence came home on the weekend she would urge him: "Speak to Wilmer Lee."

Lawrence spoke to Wilmer Lee before dinner. "What's all this?" he wanted to know. "Emily's upset," said Wilmer Lee. Lawrence said he could see that but why. They settled into one of their discussions during which the main subject got mislaid. Wilmer

Lee got to talking about Brooke's Place, the downtown bar he usually went to. His father thought it sounded interesting and wanted to know who he saw there. Wilmer Lee went into a list of names not recognizable until he reached one who had a father Lawrence knew. They fell to talking about that one. With Wilmer Lee you never got anywhere.

After the hospital job, Emily had traveled for a firm which distributed cosmetics made in France to department stores everywhere. She had to use the line and sing its praises. She hoped for a trip to France, but her sales were not high enough. In one of her stops in Charlottesville, she met Lawrence. She thought he worked in the store and was going into her spiel, but he was only on his way to the men's room. Passing through cosmetics, he had stopped to sniff an aftershave. She took him for the manager. It was an honest mistake. He used to say she picked him up. Off on her journey through the Blue Ridge Mountains, next stop Roanoke, she thought of the way he had cocked his head and smiled at her when she confessed her mistake. He said later that on his journey to Washington, he thought of her.

It was a happy occurrence for them both. Lawrence Hafner's wife had died; Emily Marshall was divorced. She had a grown son, Tim, who was invariably off somewhere. Lawrence had those three sons and a father, all clustered at home. At times she thought he married her to look after them. Was she glad or sorry? They took up a lot of time, but time was all she had. When introduced they joined hands and danced around her. "You can be mama," Wilmer Lee crowed. And they echoed with delight, "She's our mamma! Hi, Mamma!" They called her Emily. Mr. Earl said with dignity, "It's nice you're here." "You bet it is," said Lawrence.

Then she went in the kitchen and they all waited for their dinner.

◆

The very evening after Milton went to the grocery, Lawrence came home unexpectedly. It was only Thursday and he was not due till Friday. After Milton had shopped, Emily had cooked, Wilmer Lee had not only showed up but also took a shower before dinner. Last to appear was Hubert. Mr. Earl got lifted into his usual place at table. He looked satisfied as he saw them all there. He glanced about and tapped his glass. Grace. "Lord make us thankful . . ."

"New deal in the works," said Lawrence. "I'm closing in." Lawrence sold package insurance deals to large firms. This one was a clothing chain. Emily knew about it. He had been scouting around about a similar project the day he ran into her. "I've pulled off a bit. Let 'em think about it."

"No use breathing down their necks," said Hubert wisely, repeating what he'd often heard.

"What's at school?" Lawrence asked Hubert.

"Fraternity mess."

"Why a mess?"

"Because it always is."

"You wanted to join."

"Only way to stay in school. Don't join, you're a bum."

"We can't have bums," said Lawrence.

Mr. Earl said his days in a fraternity had been a pleasure. The boys were great friends. In those days everybody was a friend. Such fine boys.

"In my day," said Lawrence, "they kept a file of themes you could copy for your assignments."

"But you never did it," Emily said, hoping to be right.

"Tempted," said Lawrence, helping himself to chicken and rice.

Milton then spoke up and talked a long time. He said that at school some people copied their geometry problems. He thought they were like puzzles and he liked to get the answer for himself. If you copied you didn't ever see how they worked. They worked like a piece of machinery getting in gear . . . "huruuup! haruup! click . . . click . . ." There was one that you had to do by getting the square root of a hard number like four hundred and twenty-eight . . .

Wilmer Lee whooped. "I always wondered about the square root of four hundred and twenty-eight."

"It's crucial!" shouted Hubert.

"How can I live without it!" shouted Wilmer Lee.

"I'll never pass chemistry!"

"My girlfriend will dump me!"

Milton stopped. He got angry. He got hurt. "Show it to me after supper, Milton," Lawrence offered.

"Okay," said Milton, in a small voice.

Emily was pleased. Kindness pleased her.

So what better life was there, she thought, as the boys cleared up and stacked the dishwasher. Sometimes, horsing around, they broke a plate. Tonight they didn't. She bent to kiss Milton's blond head. He grinned. What better life than to be important to all of them?

She wondered about it aloud at her bridge club. She wondered to herself when writing to her wandering son Tim. Tim never answered and might by now be at a new address. When she complained about Wilmer Lee, Lawrence would tell her that at least he was better than Tim. She didn't like being told that. Lawrence did not know Tim. He idolized his boys.

She could talk freely at her bridge club.

"No, I love them all. I really do. I get tired at times, but somehow all I do for them is fun." (She thought of Hubert coming into her room to read her a section of an essay he had written for his history class. They both thought it was great.)

"You could take a trip," Sarah Livsey said. (Emily thought of Wilmer Lee, sitting in the bedroom, watching her recline, full of lustful thoughts. "What do you think about when Daddy's not here?" "I think about him." That shooed him off.)

She was smiling. "A trip? Lawrence wouldn't like that. We couldn't leave them alone."

"With Hubert home for a week, they wouldn't be alone."

"There's nowhere I want to go."

Sara Livsey dealt cards. "Think of somewhere," she advised.

Helena Roberts said that personally where she'd love to go was Aspen, Colorado. She and Louis had been there once. It was divine.

Mary Sue just wanted to go anywhere at all and do nothing.

Emily shuffled and dealt. To be needed, to be understood. That for her was all.

◆

"Mr. Earl," said Emily the next afternoon, "you know I love all of you, don't you?"

"Why certain thing," said Mr. Earl, looking up from the paper.

"Do you love all of us?" she wanted to know.

"Equally? I don't know if anybody can love equally." He turned the huge leaves and straightened them out. "I love just the way it is," he concluded, and she thought that was the way she felt too. Day followed day in what you might call harmony. That was to say that expected things happened as expected.

Blackie lay nearby, head on her paws, watching Emily. "Good dog," said Mr. Earl. Blackie thumped her tail.

2.

Though going somewhere was not what Emily would have decided to do, the very next week she got a sudden, unexpected chance when a letter arrived from her ex-husband Jeffrey. There was also a message from Jeffrey on Lawrence's cell phone, which he called from Richmond to transmit it to her. She might have wondered why Jeffrey didn't call her directly, but talking with Lawrence first was politic and softened the response area. Jeffrey hated to appeal for anything, but now that he wanted to, he went all the way around elbow to thumb. He was very sick and wanted to see her. Just once more, was the nub of the message. So the letter said also.

Emily called Lawrence. "When you get home, we'll talk about it."

Lawrence said he wouldn't be home so soon, and what if Jeffrey died.

Jeffrey dying? At times she almost wished he would. He kept her from Tim. She was sure of that, but couldn't prove it.

"Well, I'll just speak to him," she told Lawrence. And she did.

"Jeffrey? This is Emily."

"Emily," said Jeffrey, "I'm about to die." The hoarse prickly quality of his voice was same as ever. It reminded her of rough wool.

"Lawrence said you wanted me to call."

"I want you to come here. I want to see you. You'll do that, won't you?"

"What's wrong with you, Jeffrey?"

"Same as ever. It just got worse. If you think it ain't so, you can call the doctor."

"You've got Mildred."

"Mildred's fine, but it's you I need to speak to. Personally."

"I'll think about it."

"There's no time to think. Just say you will."

She must have promised because here she was packing. Hubert was back at college. Mr. Earl would have to manage with Wilmer Lee and Milton. She left some beef stew in the refrigerator. Anybody could make rice or potatoes and cut up a salad, even Wilmer Lee. Furthermore, Wilmer Lee and Mr. Earl got on fine. It was mainly that Wilmer Lee didn't like to keep a schedule or come home early. He liked to go to the movies on impulse. He hung out.

"You'll have to feed Blackie." It was coming over her how much she did, every day.

"Grandpa will remind me."

"You and Milton can shop."

"Got no money!" Wilmer Lee sang in a sort of triumph, trying to make everything difficult.

"I'll leave you some. For groceries."

Milton walked in, finger in a book. "I heard he was sick, but what's his name?"

She wanted to shake him. Maybe she would be glad to get away for a while.

◆

Emily drove well and liked it. She admired the tilt and lean of the big highways, speeding on through the flatlands, fields on either side, then the low forested hills, rising toward the mountains.

Was there need to hurry? Jeffrey had a recurrent lung problem, often stifling his breath, but sometimes leading to radiation and thence to hospital stays. He had smoked himself into it: everyone knew that. He also had Mildred, a nice enough divorcée who ran a clothing shop on the main street of Congreve, their small city. They spent their weekends together. He said she was a good companion. But what about Tim?

The traffic had thinned. On her right a long stretch of hillside dropped suddenly off into a valley, where a narrow stream curved through. She glimpsed a road sloping down, edging slowly toward the stream. Then all of it vanished as she passed.

What if she went back and explored on her own? What if she never showed up for Jeffrey or Tim? Then she could go calmly back to Lawrence and Hubert and Wilmer Lee and Milton and Mr. Earl? Then did she just tell lies?

She drove on.

3.

Responding to needs at home, Lawrence now returned every evening he could make it. That was about every other evening. His business range worked up through Virginia and sometimes down into South Carolina, but as a rule, close to home.

Sometimes he helped Milton and Wilmer Lee warm up leftover food, sometimes they sent out for pizza or Chinese. Wilmer Lee remarked that if it wasn't for Grandaddy they could all go out and eat. Lawrence agreed that was true. Emily rang up. Jeffrey was better. Tim was there. She sounded—well, how did she sound? Mr. Earl wanted to know. Lawrence couldn't quite say.

The second time Lawrence came home, Mr. Earl called him aside into his own room and asked him to shut the door.

◆

The house Emily had come to looked the same as ever, one story brick and clapboard, set off from a medium-sized town almost but not quite in the mountains. The yard was not tended, some trash needed picking up, and a flower bed near the front porch struggled to live. She knocked and heard a weak call. Going in, she heard, "Come look for me. Hide-and-seek."

Emily well knew that talking to Jeffrey was irritating, whether he was dying or not. Now he was half-teasing. He liked to worry people, especially her. Grown very thin, he sat in a wheelchair with a blanket pulled up high. She asked if he was cold.

He replied that he sometimes wondered. "Nobody to complain to. All day sometimes. Nobody to try being around me. But I really don't want anybody. Just Tim."

His gray hair, still thick, hung over his forehead. He sat slumped forward, his long face made longer by letting his mouth droop in a slack way. He kept looking down.

"Why haven't you married Mildred?"

"She didn't want to."

"Well then there's only Tim. Or you can hire somebody."

"Paying for company," he grumbled. He was hooked up through his nose to a machine that sat on the floor beside him and purred. Out of nowhere, Tim walked into the room. "Mamma." It was all he said. They hugged.

Tim was a substantial-looking boy, now grown to just before manhood, neither short nor tall. He had thick wavy light hair, worn close as if he had bought it and put it on. Emily, proud of him, stroked his head.

In the afternoon Jeffrey and Tim played country music. Jeffrey strummed quite ably on a guitar; he had picked it up late in life to humor Tim. Tim blew on his flute. He had always been attached to it. She would have loved to sit and listen and simply be near him. She remembered his early days, how warm and lively. They had all been happy or so she had wanted to think. But Jeffrey's drinking put him beside himself, mean, remote, sneering. She left with Tim, went back to business jobs. She knew how to arrange life. She advanced. Tim made high grades.

"I still miss someone . . ." An old Johnny Cash song. They didn't sing the words, but she remembered them. She sat smiling, watching Tim. The way he sat on the floor, half squatting on folded legs and piping, made her remember something she'd read, a myth figure, young, near some woods. Jeffrey banged his fist on the guitar and broke the mood.

◆

Back home at that moment, Lawrence came into his father's room and shut the door.

"What is it, Daddy?"

"It's Wilmer Lee. He brought this girl in last night. I heard them."

"Umm," said Lawrence.

"She left mighty late. It could have been around two o'clock."

Lawrence sighed. Now he'd have to talk to Wilmer Lee.

He found him on the terrace Emily had closed in with windows and lined with plants. The plants needed water. Wilmer Lee was sitting in front of the TV. He was reading a magazine, not watching anything. Lawrence snapped off the picture.

"What's this Grandaddy's telling me?"

Wilmer Lee looked up. He put down the magazine. "About what?"

"I imagine you know," said Lawrence. "That girl."

"She came in to borrow a CD. I thought she was going right out. Anyway she didn't stay long."

"Just pretty late?"

"She ain't here now." Wilmer Lee grinned. Suddenly he had turned their talk into something man-to-man. It was a neat trick. Lawrence pulled back from it. He became a father.

"I won't have this. Just because Emily's gone you needn't think—"

"It won't happen again. I promise."

Wilmer Lee tilted back his dark head in an honorable way. He was about to speak.

"She was black." They both looked up and there stood Milton. "You little devil," said Wilmer Lee. "She was no such thing."

"I saw her," said Milton.

Lawrence said, "Black, white, or purple, I won't have this."

"Yes, sir," said Wilmer Lee. He went uptown and did not appear for dinner.

During the afternoon Milton went in to see his grandfather, who was asleep, sitting in his accustomed chair. He was snoring. Milton wanted to wake him and climb up on his lap. Blackie was asleep too. Milton lay down beside the dog and lifted one paw to rest over him. Blackie pulled back the paw and growled. Milton went into his own little room, a sort of large closet they had fixed up for him when Emily came. Before that, he slept on a bunk in Lawrence's room. Here, though, he could keep his books. They

were outgrowing the two shelves, but okay so far. He had the novels all together, poetry next and then books about history and people. At times he tried to decide which one he liked best. Now,
feeling forlorn, he ran his finger along the familiar spines and
thought how much he loved them all. He lay down on his bunk and
all of a sudden he turned over on his face and started crying. That
girl wasn't black; he didn't know why he said that. Emily had left
them. He was sure she wouldn't come back. She wanted to go. She
didn't love them. He cried until he got tired of it. Then he slept.

4.

"You can stay here with me," said Jeffrey. "I think those people
work you too hard."

Emily laughed. "Don't you realize? I married Lawrence."

"You married me, too. But then you left."

"We agreed on it. You went out to work, came home to drink.
I had to escape."

"Left me to die alone. Smart, wasn't it."

"You weren't even sick then."

"I am now."

"Jeffrey, do you think all this is just a joke?" But she was laughing, too.

"I always had fun with you," he said. "Let's laugh some more.
Remember the time we lost Tim?"

"Not lost, mislaid, you said."

"Still is."

Mildred came with dinner from a restaurant, packed in cartons. Mildred was brisk and competent. She wore samples of the clothes she sold. The pantsuit she had on was green. "It sold better in black," she remarked, and said it was an Oscar Perle. "He'll have to have somebody," she confided in Emily. "You can't stay on indefinitely. I personally think he could do more on his own. Disconnect for maybe five hours a day. He won't try it. I think it scares him."

"Drinking?" asked Emily.

"Just one or two. In the evening. Well, you saw."

"We can try to persuade him to disconnect," said Emily, "but I doubt it would work."

From three rooms away, Jeffrey heard. "Disconnect! She wants to kill me."

"I want to help," Emily hastened to explain. "Get you breathing on your own."

He shouted that he didn't believe her.

She came and sat beside him. "Jeffrey, why did you want me here?"

"The old times," he said. "Tim," he said.

"What's this about dying?"

"I have to do it sometime," he chuckled.

"So does everybody."

"Why not now?"

Jeffrey had been an insurance adjuster. He gave valuable witness in lawsuits. He knew how to fix blame where it was deserved. Awarded with ample bonuses, he took her on trips—the West Coast, Mexico. She thought of those trips as green little atolls sticking up in a sea which was liquid but was not water.

Even now, Jeffrey wasn't able to put off his sardonic mask. It was how he fended off life, she thought. If he changed, he'd be lost from himself. So she reasoned it, and kept hoping for a sign for three whole days of something better, which she could not stir into life.

"He's not dying," said Mildred. "He's just the same as ever."

That night Emily packed up to return. The next morning she left her room vowing to make one more try. She found Jeffrey slumped in his chair. He had died as he said he would, a final winning gesture.

◆

Tim snuffled back his tears and she soothed him. At least she had a breakthrough there. Mildred, who knew everybody in town, made the funeral arrangements. It seemed odd she never cried. *You'd think they had a business arrangement*, Emily thought.

"You can come back with me," Emily told Tim. "You couldn't live in the house but you could find a place near us. There're bands there too."

"Don't want to," said Tim.

"Then how will you live? You'll have what he left you, but no job in sight."

"I play with Will Parker's band. I do tenor sax. We travel some."

"What money do they take in?"

"Not much. They've got hopes."

She sighed. Were hopes enough?

Tim stood up tall. "You ain't responsible for me."

"Maybe not. But I love you."

"Don't you love all them over there?"

"I do, yes."

Tim asked her to come and see his hideout.

The two rooms toward the third floor back of a rather scruffy brick apartment building on a little-used street were disorderly, with corner windows and sunlight. She smelled pot. She cleaned some dirty glasses, then arranged the papers and books. She propped a trombone in the corner and placed a clarinet and flute side by side on a chair. Music sheets lay sprawled on the bed. He sat on the bed and watched her, smiling. She reminded herself that he was a man now, not her hopelessly boyish son. He used to quarrel so. Once in exasperation she had said, "Oh, go back to your father!" "Okay, I will," he'd answered, and to her surprise, did it.

"Why didn't you stay over with him?" she asked.

"This is for my music. He paid for it."

"Now he's left you the house."

He picked up the clarinet and put it in her hands. "Play something. Run a scale."

Laughing, she put the reed in her mouth and blew. It squawked. She had studied piano as a child and could try again. More successful, she ran a scale.

Tim was excited. "See! You could."

"Could what?"

"Learn a little bit. Come play with us. Maybe you could sing. We'll dress you up cute. You'd like 'em. We got trombone, double bass. Rod's trying to find an electric piano. You could play that."

She set the clarinet down carefully. "Listen, baby boy. Just let me hear from you."

◆

On the return drive, she stopped beside the highway, got out and looked back at the small city where he had always lived—the handsome young man she had married on a sunny day in Georgia. That week in Savannah she would always remember. *I should have mentioned Savannah*, she thought. It was too late.

5.

Mr. Earl was happy she was home. Blackie pawed her skirt until she patted her head. Hubert came home from college for the weekend, just to see her, he said. "We didn't know what you were doing over there," he told her, and was only partly joking. Lawrence, having closed a good business deal, stayed home every night and coddled her. He called her his Dumpling: she was small and almost plump, easy to hold. They made love slowly, with considerable pleasure. Concluding, he murmured, "It's close to perfect." Sliding contented into sleep, she knew it was the whole of the household he meant.

Next morning: "You see how we've counted on you," he said, over and over. Wilmer Lee brought her a box of candy. Milton told her all his complaints.

Mr. Earl asked how her son was. "He wants to travel with a band," she answered. Mr. Earl said "Ummm."

She sat down with Mr. Earl and thought it over. "He wanted me to stay with him," she said. "His father left him everything, including the house. He said I could live in it while he came and went with the band."

Mr. Earl put down his paper. His anxious face, his deep wrinkles creasing. "Did you want to?"

She thought of Tim's serious look, strained. "I hate to lose him." She paused. "This life is fine for me."

She had to go to the grocery and then cook supper. She called to Milton to go with her.

The front yard of Lawrence's house was a long stretch down to a row of trees. The backyard was narrow, but sloped into a thicket of small trees and brush. Why did anyone build a house so far back on the lot? Lawrence said he hadn't planned it and didn't know. Emily often stood at the door and watched the light fade through the trees. And in that very light, who should appear a week later, but Tim.

❖

He came walking through the trees at twilight, up the long front yard, carrying a guitar, his father's no doubt, with a few other instruments tied together and carried on his back.

"Hi Mama." He gave her a sidelong kiss and walked through the front door without being asked.

Mr. Earl was in the living room. "Where are you going, young man?' he asked.

"I just came to see Mamma," said Tim. He was tired and sat down. "I'm Tim."

"I doubt if you walked all the way," said Mr. Earl, who wished he would go.

"No, sir. I got a ride."

Emily, feeling dizzy, put an extra plate on the table. At dinner, the boys did not seem to think Tim was there. Milton, however, did pass dishes to him, and Wilmer Lee looked straight at him once to remark, "She belongs to us now." He grinned but meant it too. Tim ate, eyes on his plate, and didn't reply. Hubert was away at school. Emily hoped Lawrence would return soon.

After dinner, she sat down with Tim in a side room off the entranceway.

"You must miss him," she said. "Is that why you came?"

"It seemed like the next thing to do."

"I wish I had mentioned Savannah."

"Who's Savannah?"

"It's where we got married. He was best then." She laughed. "Maybe we both were."

"You must have been good sometime. You had me."

They both laughed. And when that happened they both felt at home together. She fixed him a bunk bed in the basement.

Two days later a car drove up and a strange young man got out. Tim and he carried in a number of instruments—saxophone, trombone, even some small drums. Emily was frantic for a while, but recalled an unused storage hut in the backyard near the bamboo hedge. Tim was persuaded. By the time Lawrence got home, it was all done. They had taken old magazines and papers to a dumpster, thrown out two broken chairs, moved in the bunk bed, and cleaned the two windows. With rain coming on, Mr. Earl napped in his room with Blackie and scarcely heard their comings and goings. The strange young man drove away.

When Lawrence got home the next day, he did not remark on anything, but he thought about it, Emily could tell. They dined on lamb roast with carrots, potatoes, and peas. While the boys washed up, she prepared a plate, out of sight in the kitchen. But Lawrence observed her.

"Oh, is he still here?" And when she explained, "Why didn't you ask him in?"

"Tomorrow I will. But he wanted to stay out. I think we should talk about it."

"So do I," Lawrence agreed.

Upstairs they sat with the bedroom door closed. "This is a strange predicament," said Lawrence. "You care for him, you want to help him. But what about the rest of us?"

"I didn't know he was coming. I don't think he will stay long."

"But you don't know."

"No, I don't."

"Why don't you ask him?"

"I will."

"What's he sleeping on?"

"I moved out the bunk bed from the basement. He washes at the outside hydrant. He goes to the bathroom in the woods. It's not much of a way to live, I know."

"You've got to bring him in. I can't have this."

"He's got these instruments. His own and those that boy brought. Drums, a saxophone, trombone. That clarinet, that flute.

I don't know what all. He wants to play all the time. The boys would simply rebel. And poor Mr. Earl."

"I'll talk to him. I'll find him a place in town. Then he can get a job. You can visit him. By the way, you don't think he's gay?"

She started. "I never thought that."

"Hubert mentioned it. He thinks he is."

"Then tell Hubert he's wrong."

Lawrence went out for a talk with Tim but couldn't find him. He had evidently gone off somewhere.

Lawrence left early the next morning without talking to Tim. He kissed her goodbye with a laugh. "You're in a cage of wild animals," he said.

◆

Two days later, Lawrence still gone, she was relieved to be getting dressed to go for bridge.

"Lord, how much can you stand?" asked Sarah Livsey.

"You ought to turn them all out," said Helena.

"What a menagerie," said Mary Sue. "You married the whole county."

"I care about them all," said Emily, and made five clubs.

When she drove into the yard, Blackie came out to greet her. She saw that Blackie had something to tell: she did not wag.

Tim was in the kitchen red-faced and snarling. "They've taken them," he fumed. All his instruments were missing. He said it was Wilmer Lee, who presently came home and professed not to know what they were talking about. Emily had to believe him. She couldn't begin to suspect Milton. Hubert, home for the weekend, had gone to a movie, but only remarked when he returned, "We won't have to listen to all that racket." That left Lawrence, not even due back until late.

"Maybe your friend came back," she ventured to Tim. "Didn't he own some of those? Where were you?"

He was looking in the house for an extension cord for the electric heater. It was cold out there. He didn't see anybody. It was a mystery. He clung to her. "I know they don't like me." She stroked his soft hair. "They think I'm gay."

"Just say you're not."

"I did."

The next day, like the musical instruments, Tim disappeared. Nobody knew anything. He had not spoken to anyone, and had left no message.

Emily called Jeffrey's old number. It had been disconnected. She called Tim's number with the same results. She called Mildred. Mildred had nothing to offer except advice. "I wouldn't worry. He'll show up when he wants to." "He's not your son," said Emily.

Lawrence came home on the weekend and put out messages to the police. They came by and checked over the storage hut. They asked lots of questions. When they left, Lawrence sighed and went upstairs to shower before dinner. Emily, in a daze, cooked a pork roast. Hubert came in; he also showered.

It was when she sat down at the table with them all that the strange thing happened. Her place at table was next to Lawrence who sat at one end, facing Mr. Earl. So she began by turning left to Milton, then to Mr. Earl himself and straight across to Hubert and Wilmer Lee, and next a sharp right to Lawrence. Everyone had fallen silent.

Then, just like that, she knew!

"You've done it!"

Mr. Earl, about to say the blessing, stopped short. Wilmer Lee and Hubert both looked down. All were silent.

"Done what?" Lawrence asked.

"They've run him away. You know it's true."

"Who has run him away?"

"They all have. They know it."

"I didn't," said Milton.

"Shut up," said Wilmer Lee.

"It was those dadgum others," said Mr. Earl. "I had to stop 'em, Blackie and me—"

"What is all this?" Lawrence demanded.

Milton started eating his dinner.

"After dinner," Lawrence said, "we're going right in the study."

They knew what that meant. And they knew who he meant— Wilmer Lee and Hubert, Milton too, and maybe Mr. Earl, maybe even Blackie. But not Emily.

It was toward dessert that she asked: "Did you hurt him?" She had sat staring at the food she had cooked for them, unable to speak or eat.

Silence again. Lowered eyes.

"It was a fight," Milton offered.

"Shut up," said Hubert.

Unhappy, they left the table. The whole house heard the study door close.

Why not ask me? Emily wondered. But Lawrence's authority had risen up and was ready for action no one could deny. Even Mr. Earl was in that room. She was left alone with Blackie, who for some reason stayed by her.

From the living room, trying to look at the news on TV, she could hear the murmur of voices, rising then lowering. Once the door flew open and out came Milton. He ran into the living room, saw and skirted her, going to stand at a window, holding the curtain, his back to her.

"What is it, honey?"

"They run me out."

So that left Lawrence, Mr. Earl, and the older boys, in the study together, men talking things out.

"Why run you out?" She caught her breath, even to ask it.

" 'Cause . . ."

She wanted to ask *'cause what*, but with slow steps, here came Mr. Earl, out too. Blackie got up and went to him. Then they turned to her, Mr. Earl sitting down, panting for breath, Blackie serious, Milton's small puffy face streaked with tears.

Eventually the study door opened and the three trooped out, Lawrence came to her. He pulled up a straight chair and sat down near her. "I've got it all straight," he said. She sat and listened.

"Them little bastards," said Mr. Earl. "I ran 'em out."

"Yes, well, we can start with that," Lawrence said. He spoke to Emily.

"When Tim's two friends started hanging out with him to practice, they came in the house once or twice while you were gone . . . to play bridge, to the grocery . . . I don't know. Anyway, they were looking for a snack out of the fridge or something—"

"Them little bastards," said Mr. Earl. "They got no b'iness here. Blackie and me— I saw six of them, some in the kitchen, some going upstairs. All over this house. Swarmin'."

"Daddy, please. I've got the whole thing straight now. Let me just tell Emily."

"They were kicking everything around," said Milton.

"It's time you shut up," said Hubert.

"About right fucking now," said Wilmer Lee.

"Language like that is out," their father said. "And I mean it."

Wilmer Lee said he was sorry, but just the same . . .

"I ran 'em out," said Mr. Earl. "Run 'em out with my walking cane. Me and Blackie."

"There were only two, not six. Daddy told them to go," Lawrence continued with dignity and assurance. "After that, the boys here got hold of the instruments and hid them. Tim didn't know where. He thought those boys had just gone off with theirs and his too."

"Have you hurt him?" Emily interrupted. "Is he crippled?"

"Emily! Don't be absurd."

"We were just teasing," said Hubert. "It was all like a game." He was about to go back to school and had promised to pick somebody up.

"We gave 'em back," said Wilmer Lee, who had a date in town. Reasonably Lawrence told her that the boys had returned them and that Tim had left with the saxophone and all that other stuff, to find his bunch. He had called on his cell phone. They came for him. "We'll do our best to find him. He couldn't have gone far. I was about to get a room for him in town. You must see that he was causing friction here."

That was true.

"He'll probably let you hear something. Those musical kids go around in groups, as we've learned." He laughed. "The police are on the lookout. We'll find him."

"You turned out Mr. Earl."

"You know how Daddy gets mixed up. He couldn't tell it straight to save his life. And Milton . . . He makes up everything."

Dazed, she saw the older boys depart, still amazed how they had grown since she came, how tall and brusque they had become, how assertive they were around their father. Even a bit taller. *He believes them. He adores them.*

She did not follow Lawrence upstairs. She did not move from the couch. Ready for bed, he called her from the stair. "Come on, Dumpling," he said. He came down to her. "I know how you feel. He's your boy. But we'll find him. You'll see." "Just let me alone awhile," she said. He kissed her cheek and drew away, returning upstairs, leaving her to her thoughts. Lawrence was a nice man.

Soon Mr. Earl hobbled through for letting Blackie out. He regarded her, lying on the couch. "What's happened?" he asked. "It's what I'd like to know," she said. He considered. "We'll ask Blackie," he said, and that was as good as any, she thought, as Blackie went out and then returned. "Don't worry," said Mr. Earl.

"He's bound to come back." He went to bed in his downstairs room off the kitchen.

She lay there alone until Milton ventured down at midnight, in pajamas, barefoot. He knelt on the floor and put his chin over the arm of the couch, eyes fixed on her. "They beat him up," said Milton. "They said if he came back, they'd kill him. They said he better get gone forever. And ever. And ever. They said——"

"Oh, Milton, stop it."

"They got me to watch for when you came back. All the time you were gone, they made me watch. They did that every time."

"You minded them? Every time?"

"I thought you'd like to know how it was. I think they broke his arm. He couldn't lift his guitar. They hit his jaw. He couldn't play his trumpet."

"He didn't have a trumpet. He had a saxophone."

"Then he couldn't play that either. It was his jaw. It was bleeding. It had blood——"

"Milton! You make things up."

"But suppose I don't?" said Milton.

She buried her face in a cushion. "Go back to bed."

When she looked again, he was still there, his chin hooked over the chair arm. "I love you," he said.

Emily thought, *There must be such a thing as a truthful liar.*

His small devil face still stared at her. She must have slept or dozed. Milton was gone. She must have dreamed. She went wandering through the dark streets of her own mind. Those distant long-ago times. She ran into Dr. Ferguson, whose assistant she had been, at the hospital. "You know," he told her, "that order you signed by mistake was my fault. I should have looked at it." "You were in the storage room screwing that nurse. I was angry. I signed it fast." A hundred electronic appliances for cauterizing, useful in delicate surgeries. It should have been ten. All down the line, the order was passed along. The great expense stunned the hospital. A mistake, an accident. *But I did it—it was my fault* . . . Then she was in Savannah with Jeffrey, looking out the hotel window at two boys scuffling on the street below. Jeffrey took sides. "The one in the blue shirt is going to win," he said. "Bet you five." But in the end both boys were sprawled out on the pavement, traffic stalled, and a cop came to get them up, while from the window Jeffrey and Emily applauded. They exchanged five-dollar bills laughing, and then made love. While she slept Jeffrey went down to the bar. Now she was in a dim childhood, her mother at the sewing machine, her father somewhere near calling "Where are you?" Answering "Here," her mother answering "Here." Now she was in a long corridor and far down at a door something was scratching on the wood. She moved toward it.

◆

Alone in bed Lawrence drowsed and turned. He heard Wilmer Lee come in and Milton scurry to his cubbyhole. But nothing else. He had to go to Charlotte on business. He was struggling to keep Hubert in school. He should hire a housekeeper. He had let Emily do too much. She had said she wanted to. And his boys . . . they

wanted her. He counted on them . . . his wonderful boys. Of course
he did. Of course . . .

Finally he rose and went downstairs. The couch and the room
were empty. Lawrence felt he had swallowed a large chunk of ice.
Should he call, rush to the door, run to the yard? He stood frozen
in place. The kitchen! "Emily!"

Sure enough, the kitchen door was open and presently she
came in from the dark with Blackie by her side.

She had opened the door to the scratching she heard, and there
was Blackie.

"But you've been out already," she had said, and letting the dog
out the kitchen door stepped out herself into the night air. There
down the slope where Blackie was heading she saw the bare outline
in the dark. "Tim!" She ran. He ran toward her.

They went at once to the shack and huddled out there in the
dark. His face was swollen, up near his eye. He was not hurt bad,
he said. Had a tooth knocked loose.

"What else? Did they threaten you?" "Said I had to go," he
admitted. "I went off with the bunch. I don't want to come back
anyway. They hate me. Especially that Hubert. I just came for my
flute." He nosed around till he found it, dropped in a corner.

"But what happened?" She had to know.

"They played around with all my music things. That Wilmer
started blowing on my trombone. I grabbed it but he pushed me
with it. I fell down and hit my cheek, right there. But then they
threw them at me. And laughed at me. I tried to fight and then I
heard the car. It was Will Parker come for me. I yelled for him and

we got stuff together from where they threw them. They had got mud on the sax and bent the trombone and didn't care. It was Hubert; he was the worst. 'Don't tell me you're leaving us?' was what he said. 'Leaving for good,' I said. And Wilmer said, 'I'll cry and cry,' and Hubert said, 'I'll shoot myself. I'll die.' They kept laughing. Laughing all the time."

The shack seemed another country, far away. "You want to stay on here?" he asked. "You want to come with us? I could teach you some more. You could learn fast." He sat on the floor and ran a scale and smiled at her. She saw his resemblance to Jeffrey and remembered the day, soon after they met, how they were drinking martinis in a Charleston bar and he said, "Come on now. Let's go to Savannah." "Why Savannah?" "Get married in Savannah. It's a good enough place." His smile was beguiling. She saw that smile again.

"Traveling around with a band? What would you do with me?"

"I'm telling you. We'd think of something." They hugged.

"Just let me hear from you," she pleaded. Cell phone! With promises and hugs, he wrote the number for her. A car was waiting, far down the drive. "We've got the bass in the back," he boasted. "We keep looking for an electric piano. Something you can play." It was a good enough fantasy for the moment.

She and Blackie returned to the house.

Entering the kitchen, finding Lawrence . . .

"I wouldn't have seen him except for Blackie. Except for her I would never have seen him at all." She would always believe that.

"I was afraid you were gone," he said.

"Gone?" she repeated, but knew that when she heard the car

start and pull away, some of her went with it. She stood on firm ground. She took a deep breath and told him. She repeated all that Tim had told her, every bit. The blows, the jeers. Oh yes, his boys. They had done that.

Lawrence was shaken. He stared at Blackie, who sat scratching behind her ear. Like a thrown ball, she had brought these woes to light. Helplessly, he looked at Emily. She saw the trouble in his firm, trustful face. "Don't go."

"Oh, I'm still here. Honest ones have to stick together."

She smiled encouragement, knowing they had entered a new chapter. She had had, after all, so much practice.

Christmas Longings

The front door slammed for what must be the twentieth time that night. Elaine Avery put her hands to her ears. "Margie, can't you . . . ?"

No, Margie couldn't. "It even smells like snow!" she proclaimed, running to the fire to warm up again.

"You are worrying your mother," George Avery advised from behind his paper.

That was when Sonia piped up. "I'm going to be an angel! I'm going to be an angel!"

It was the church pageant she meant. Last year she had been a little one. This year, she could be in the bigger group. For the Smithville Presbyterian Church came alive with angels every Christmas. One appeared to a pretty high school girl, Tina Jenkins, who for one night plus practices was the Virgin Mary. Some made a chorus and sang to the shepherds. And some, with shining tinsel around their heads, balancing wings, softly sang "Away in a Manger." That was near the cradle where little baby Jesus was a light glowing inside.

Sonia jumped up and down just to think of it. It would be another week. Her sister Margie would give up the whole pageant for one good snowfall. Outside, in the fresh cold air she had stood with her face lifted to the heavens. She thought she had felt a flake touch her cheek.

Smithville was the last little town in the middle section of the state before the mountains soared up in the west. In the daytime you could see what was now true both day and night, the pure white layer high above. Each day it came a little lower, white, spilled down from heaven. But not to Smithville yet. Margie was cross. She took it out on her little sister Sonia. "If you an angel, you got be sweet."

"I *am* sweet!" Sonia said back.

"No you're not. You're mean!"

"I am *not* mean. Am I, Mamma?"

"Angels can't be mean. You can't be an angel!"

By now they were shouting again. George Avery put down his paper. "It's time for bed." He also had to shout to be heard.

Elaine Avery put down her Bible and the book she read to help her understand it. She had been brought up by a family descended from Scots. They were strict Calvinist Presbyterians and believed everything the Bible said was true. She was trying to get up her Sunday school lesson for tomorrow. She taught the class.

"Angels are not necessarily sweet or mean either. One thing they are is obedient. They do what they are told."

"Who tells them?" Sonia asked.

"God tells them and they do it. Sometimes it's not so sweet."

The girls had grown silent. Their mother knew about these things. She had even begun to study for the ministry when she met and married Daddy.

"One has a flaming sword," said Margie, with awe in her voice that came from what she had learned and believed. "To keep us out of paradise."

"They've got wings," said Sonia.

"Not necessarily," Elaine said. "Sometimes they just look like anybody else. You wouldn't know they were angels at all."

Both the girls grew quiet. They were fighting off sleep, the way children do.

"What else do they do?" Sonia asked.

"They climb ladders," said their mother.

"And go to bed when they're told to," their father said.

"Have you ever seen one?' asked Margie.

"I might have. One might pass me on the street. I wouldn't know if he was an angel." Now she was laughing at them, her beautiful little girls.

"It could be a girl angel," Sonia put in.

"I bet they don't go to bed," said Margie. "They're too busy."

"But little girls have to," Elaine said, still laughing.

So finally they did.

In the morning they all dressed for Sunday School. There was still no snow. Dressed in their best dresses, coats, and snug mittens, the little girls sat together in the back of the car.

◆

For the Presbyterian Christmas pageant every year, the whole town turned out. It was well known that church gave the best one, though they had the smallest congregation next to the Episcopalians. The

Catholics, almost nonexistent, went somewhere else to church. They didn't even call it church.

There were practices. Elaine drove Sonia in so Mrs. Holcomb could tell all of them what to do. There would be Mary and Joseph, the shepherds, the angels, the wise men (Daddy would be one) and even little boys, dressed up like a donkey, a cow, two like a camel. It would all be organized.

◆

Sonia looked out the window at the soft persistent fall of New England snow. "Margie wanted snow." She recalled that day forty years before.

"Come again," her husband Lester asked. He was in an alcove bent over a new computer program.

"I was just thinking about so long ago, back in Smithville. How Margie wanted snow and how it wouldn't snow. And I wanted to be an angel."

"Well, weren't you?'

"No, it turned out I couldn't be. I had grown too tall. I had to be a shepherd and wear a dull bathrobe and carry a crook. I cried and cried. I longed to be an angel again. Like Margie wanted snow."

"Such tragedy," said Lester, and bent to his work.

"Oh, but after that Daddy and Uncle Raoul drove up in the mountains for some snow and brought it home."

Lester stopped. "I doubt you could do that. Wouldn't it melt?"

"They found an old ice cream freezer and packed the case

round with salt. Then they put snow in it and brought it home for Margie and me, Uncle Raoul and Aunt Margaret. I put on my white angel dress with a tinsel crown. Mama made me some wings out of coat hangers covered with white cloth. They all said I looked pretty. Then we all ate snow cream."

Now Lester was really listening. "What in the world is snow cream?"

"You put snow in a chilled glass and pour vanilla on it. You eat it with a spoon. Want to try?"

"No thanks. But there's plenty outdoors if you'd like some. Help yourself."

"The time has gone," she said.

Lester meditated. "You know what I think? I think you and Margie were spoiled to death. All that trip to the mountains your father took with your uncle. Bet they carried a bottle."

"Maybe. But they did it for Margie."

"All that fuss over angel clothes. Just so you'd get what you wanted."

"We sat and sang carols. But that wasn't all. When we finished the snow cream, we went outdoors. And it was snowing! It was our miracle! Our Christmas gift miracle."

Lester snorted. "Now I've quit believing you. Your parents did everything to please you, but does God do it too?"

Sonia began to wonder if it all really had happened that way. Over the years, memory had to walk over mountain peaks of joys and sorrows, glad things, bad things, public things, history, age, success and failure. Could the truth possibly get changed along the way? She was sure of everything except the snowfall. Hadn't she stood, a shivering angel? (Her mother threw a shawl around her.) And even yet, her sister's face came back to her, lifted up and happy, letting the soft flakes slide down her cheeks, catching in her lashes. And everyone, seeing her, laughed with happiness, sure they were blessed.

It must have been true. Sonia would believe it always.

The Wedding Visitor

*I*t *seemed a* good thing to do and because he hadn't come there in so long, he went slowly. Approaching the house from the road before it spiraled up the drive, he sat for a while and gave it a long look.

Like many Southern houses, the original structure was almost lost among the many extensions. There was the added side porch where everyone lived out each day, enjoying sun through the enveloping series of windows. He recalled another, earlier porch out back, screened in, added to escape the hot summer nights. They had slept under mosquito nets and hoped not to hear a wicked buzz. To one side of that, there was the kitchen with doors opening on one of two dining rooms. And up front, jutting out, a sturdy new entrance porch with a handsome hanging lamp. Inside all these tack-ons, the original house nested peacefully. It was nothing splendid, dating from the 1890s, he supposed, but sturdy, white, comfortable.

In the yard, recently mowed, the familiar trees had grown taller. He remembered climbing them.

Shifting gear, he wound up the driveway.

But where was everybody?

He went to the side porch, the family entrance, and getting no answer to his knock, he walked in.

Far in the back, a cousin named Emily saw him and jumped up. "It must be Rob Ellis!"

"It's me," he said, exchanging hugs. "I came for Norma's wedding."

"So did everybody," said Emily. "They're up at the church."

Then calmly, as they both sat down, she picked up *Time* magazine and continued reading. He felt a stir of his old childhood resentment about the odd way they treated him, but then laughed at himself. Emily had always been that way, doing what she wanted and not noticing anybody.

"Where's the groom?" he asked, not quite sure he could recall the name engraved on the handsome invitation.

"Sandy? He comes around after work."

"Do you like him?"

She had yet to look up. "He's okay." One of her sandals slipped off. She scratched her ankle with her toe. "Are you going to vote for Reagan?"

"Isn't everybody?" He had hoped to get away from politics.

"Normie's in the living room."

He began to feel peaceful, unwilling to do anything. It must be about one o'clock, time they all used to fold up after lunch at noon. They called it dinner. Nap time. He yawned. It was quiet—end-of-the-road quiet. When he stayed there in the summers, twenty years ago, Emily had not been born. He had seen her whenever he visited from law school at Ole Miss. Twenty years ago he had been twelve. Maybe then he had been a different person.

Whichever person he was, eventually walked through the hallway to the living room. Sure enough, his cousin Norma was there, sitting in a beautifully upholstered chair, her feet on a matching stool, reading a book. The room was shadowy, the blinds half-drawn. A tall lamp gave light on her page.

"Cousin Rob!" she exclaimed. She jumped up, hugged him close, and sat back down.

"I came to your wedding. Where is everybody?"

She laughed. "Off talking about me, I guess."

"Saying what?"

"Oh, I'm in the doghouse."

He looked around. The rich draperies, the beautiful chairs, the fireplace with logs ready for lighting, the flanking bookshelves. A room seldom used.

"It doesn't look much like a doghouse to me."

"The dog is me," she smiled, and filled him in. "It's because of my dress." She was wearing blue jeans and a checkered shirt. "I want to wear what I want to wear. It's *my* wedding. A beige dress, just with pleats and a slit up the side. You'd think I wanted to wear a bikini. And Aunt Alicia is coming all this way from Chicago, she and Uncle Harry. Everybody is mad at me. They're choosing up sides, but nobody much is on mine. Even Muzzy."

Muzzy was what they called her mother, his Aunt Molly. He looked at what she was reading. *Middlemarch*. Old classic. She was like that. Liked to keep ahead of them all. Along with the rest, he had mocked her. But later he admired her for it.

"Where's . . . your fiancé?" The name again escaped him.

"Sandy? Oh, he'll be along. He works with the road crew."

"He's not from here?"

"No, practically a Yankee."

All those porch nights. Before they had shortened the front porch and no longer used it (the change was blamed on the weather, TV, air-conditioning). Norma in her teens had sat in the swing every evening after supper. And regularly through the night air, the boys would come down the road, and up the drive, by ones and twos. She would sit and swing a little, while each one who came sat on the steps, or up in one of the rockers, talking and laughing. Sometimes one was allowed to sit beside her. Rob Ellis guessed that Sandy must have made it to the swing.

"How'd you meet him?"

"Daddy was helping out the road crew with town people. They didn't know where to find rooms, or where to eat. They wanted to stay over in the Delta. He got to asking them here for dinner once or twice, making suggestions, lining up their business. Sandy keeps their accounts. He started talking to me."

"Out in the swing?"

"The swing's out of date. He asked me to the picture show. He's fun. He doesn't care a bit what I wear to get married in. In fact, he'd just as soon not have a wedding in church. He's a Catholic. We'll have to do it all over again anyway. I haven't told them, so don't you tell them either."

"I always liked you," Rob Ellis said. When his own marriage broke up, he thought of coming back and finding Norma, but he never did it. Courting cousins didn't work. He lived on in Memphis. He worked for a congressman, wrote his press releases, tried (often unsuccessfully) to keep him away from booze and women. Helped him talk up Reagan for a second term, along with himself.

Norma shook back her rich dark hair. "We all liked you, too."

"I was wished on you every summer."

His father, divorced, had him in charge in the summers and plopped him down with relatives. A busy father, often on the road.

Norma said: "They're building this new highway just outside town. It's going to miss us completely. I guess you knew that."

He nodded. Once again, in the continued quiet of that place, he felt absorbed into it, his own spirit drowsing.

Norma dropped her book on the floor. "Let's have a drink."

A *drink*? Well, he had heard some passing talk about her, that way. Family disapproval. But she did smile in a lovely, conspiratorial way, as if to say, We can have fun, just you and me.

"It's too early," he said.

"Hell," said Norma. "You're just like all the rest. Don't tell them I asked you."

He promised.

She picked up her book. Then she thought to ask about Memphis and didn't hear what he said. Even with the fun gone from her face, she was still so pretty, such a candidate for happiness. The tilt of her head, her soft Mississippi drawl. Once when they were kids and fighting, he had caught a wad of her thick hair and pushed her aside and such a charge went prancing through him as he had never felt before. He wondered if she remembered.

Rob wandered toward the back of the house. There was bound

to be somebody in the kitchen. He wondered if they had the same old black cook, whose name also he had forgotten.

But then to his surprise, he ran into another extension, a tack-on he didn't know about. The door was open and there in a chair, an old lady was sitting, reading the paper. There was also a Bible, resting in her lap. Did everybody in the house do nothing but read?

"Hello? Can I come in?"

She removed some small slivers of eyeglasses which had slid down her nose and examined him.

"I'm trying to think who it is. No, don't tell me . . . Larry Ellis's boy . . . Now wait . . . Bob . . . no . . ."

"Rob," he finally said.

"Of course!" She stretched out a hand.

She sat enclosed in a long comfortable skirt, with roomy shoes peeping out below. He recalled her only vaguely. She had worked somewhere as a teacher and visited at intervals.

"I'm your cousin Marty," she supplied, helping him. "You're here about Norma."

"Her wedding, yes."

"I hope it works this time. She been lined up for it twice before, you know."

"No, I didn't know."

"Well, it never got as far as sending invitations. Always fizzled out. Something wrong, I reckon. That child is in her thirties. Don't watch out, she'll wind up an old maid like me. Nobody would want that."

Time to say something Southern-nice, but he didn't. "This is a nice room," he said.

"Mack built it for me." It was his uncle she meant, her sister's husband, owner and provider, taking care of everybody the best he could. "He wanted to keep me shut off from the rest of them, I guess." Now she was at it again, suspicious. Nobody wished her well. Nobody liked her. A theme song. "I'd no place else to go. I had to accept."

I'm sure they are glad to have you . . . he knew what he ought to say but didn't. You were supposed to compliment everybody.

"At least I don't have to see them all the time. And they're rid of me. Except for meals."

Considering everything told, she replaced her glasses. Her dress was loose over her frail shoulders. He wondered at her. She had worked all her life, but had wound up here, dependent on her sister's husband for a place to live out the rest of her years. She could have lived frugally alone. She needed family, he imagined. Company. Her intelligent eyes and trim face, bare of makeup, made him wonder why she'd never married.

"I remember your mamma. An energetic soul. Why your father left her, I never knew. Did you?"

"They couldn't get along." At times he hadn't blamed him. Fierce in her advertising work, she had hired various caretakers for her son. What if he didn't like them? Too bad. There was always school.

"This wedding . . ." said Marty. "I'll have to dress and go."

"Don't you want to?"

"I have to be with the family." She gave an instructive, school-teacherish smile. "Family is all we have, like them or not. Oh, not that I criticize. Don't tell them that."

He promised not to. The voice pursued him.

He wandered out to where the old screened porch still stood in place. Some kitchen things leaned around, broom and mop and bucket, a chair or two. He heard a humming, a hymn, out in the kitchen. He found the steps and went down into the yard, walking toward some pecan trees, now grown into a shady grove.

Somebody was out there, sitting in an old wicker chair, maybe another cousin. A dog detached from the scene, and came toward him, a bronze Lab who gave a low woof, tail waging, curious but friendly. Sniffing, then following.

"How you doin'?" the possible cousin said.

He saw a pleasant face, amiable, smiling under thick blond hair, unfamiliar in memory. There was a second wicker chair. Rob sat in it.

"Hi there." They shook hands. "I'm Rob. What cousin are you?"

"Not a cousin yet. About to be. I'm Sandy."

The bridegroom! "They said you were at work."

"Supposed to be. But I had to get the right suit. Dark. Rules all over the place."

"Normie's inside."

"Yeah, I know. They're worrying her to death."

"The dress?"

"Yeah, the dress. I don't give a happy damn. I just want Normie away from here."

"To where?"

"Anywhere."

Rob thought it wasn't a good answer. If there was an *away* there had to be a *where*. The dog lay down with a grunt. Rob leaned to stroke the low head.

"Say," said Sandy, "you like him? His name's Remus."

"Sure I do."

"You might want to keep Remus, while we're gone. We'll be taking a little trip. Maybe Florida. Why don't you?"

Rob said he didn't think so.

"Well how do I take a dog along? Maybe Normie wouldn't mind." He thought it over.

There was a rustle of gravel from the drive, a car arriving.

Now the onslaught, Rob thought. But he was wrong. The door slammed and only one arrival made his concerned way to the side door. His Uncle Mack himself. Worried. Head down. Walking inside.

Rob left Sandy, who said he thought he was better off outside. "Tell Normie I'm out here."

On to Uncle Mack. He kept a small office, tucked away, one of the bedrooms organized to harbor his files, his typewriter, his big fat checkbook.

"Why," he exclaimed, "if it isn't Rob. How's the boy?"

The pleasure seemed genuine. In the past, it always seemed Uncle Mack was cordial to him because he had to be. He was obliged to fulfill his duty toward his brother, who had this boy nobody knew what to do with. Especially in the summers. They stood awkwardly in the hall.

"Old Stockton working you hard?"

So he had kept up enough to know about the congressman.

"Keeping schedules. Writing speeches." Rob could have continued, but something about his uncle's presence stopped him. MacKenzie Ellis was an imposing man, a strong face above a thickened body, its heavy waistline always buttoned up in a cream-colored vest which might be satin or heavy cotton or wool.

"Supports Reagan, I guess. Up in Tennessee I'd probably vote for him. Come in."

In the office Uncle Mack sat down at his desk, then leaned his head forward on his hand, frowning.

"Where is everybody?" Rob asked again.

Uncle Mack started. "Oh, they all went up to decorate the church. Then they went over to Gert Henderson's, I imagine to talk about it all and drink coffee. Then the rehearsal and after that we go to the club for dinner." He let out a sigh.

It was two o'clock, and the sense of things to come was in the air. Uncle Mack swiveled. He had a struggle going on behind his eyes. He needed to confide. But with Rob Ellis? He scarcely ever saw the boy, clearly not a boy any longer. A man with a political job, or something like it. But not so deeply in the family he was apt to run around telling secrets. So not too big a risk. Decision.

"I'm telling you, Rob. I'm upset."

"Yes, sir."

"You may know this guy here with the road people. Milton Ward?"

"No, sir."

"I thought you might. I think he knows Stockton. He's from Memphis. Well, he runs the bunch making the new highway. I helped them all quite a bit. Just this morning he told me."

"Told you what?"

"That boy's about to be my son-in-law. And do you know what? He's been helping himself to the road crew's expense money!"

"He's right out in the backyard," Rob said.

"Where's Norma?"

"In the living room. Reading a book."

Uncle Mack let out a groan. "And now we're supposed to have this wedding. He's going to marry her!"

"I know. It's what I came for."

"Do I stop it? What do I do?" Then he added in a voice that broke, "I want her to be happy."

"So do I," Rob said. He had never imagined his uncle crying. "Maybe it's not true," he ventured.

"Oh, it's true all right. But how'd he expect to get by with it? And how much was it? Ward didn't tell me. Just said forget it. But how can I let her do it? Marry a thief?"

He suddenly rose. "Now you listen here . . ." Rob stood as well, and confronting that heavyset tower of a man, he felt like a dwarf. He had never grown tall. He was a little guy and he got even smaller when his uncle caught his lapels and all but lifted him off the floor.

"Don't you tell any of this! You hear me? I have to face it alone. It's up to me!"

Rob promised, reflecting that everybody so far, excepting Emily, had asked him not to tell something. It was as bad as politics.

From the front came a grinding crunch of gravel followed by a car door slam, steps on the walk, at the door, a welcoming call from Emily. Norma must be gone from the living room. Stamp of feet and the usual passage toward the big side porch. Emily would have to part with Ronald Reagan and *Time* magazine. Cries of greeting.

"May the Lord help me," said Uncle Mack. "I've got to greet them."

The bunch of cousins were talking loud. They were staying at the Homestead Inn . . . my, it was nice as could be . . . and where on earth was Molly (some said Muzzy), and where was Norma (some said Normie).

Rob listened and decided not to appear, be identified, screamed over, kissed and pounded. He crept through the house, tending toward the back, but did not escape running into the cook, big black Louise (he remembered the name), who knew him at once. "Lawd, Mister Rob, you ain't grown a inch."

He must have said something, escaping, looking toward the back where he had left Sandy. But Sandy now had Norma with him, standing, his arm around her, her hand resting on him, and the way they tilted Rob knew this was real to them and right. Remus seemed to know it too. He lay contentedly at their feet, as though already in a house they lived in. It seemed to grow up around them. Rob walked forward until they looked up.

"The cousins," he said to Norma. "I think it's Maud Oakley and that gang. They come by four and sixes," he explained to Sandy.

"Oh God, it's my bridesmaids!" Norma ran toward the house.

"Listen," he said to Sandy. His tone was not to be mistaken. Sandy listened. "How much did you take?"

In no more than a half a minute Sandy guessed what he meant.

"God," he said, "they never look at that account."

"Well they have now."

"Just for my dark suit. And the trip to Florida. I thought they wouldn't look."

"They've told Uncle Mack." He paused to let this be digested, then asked, "Where can we find them?"

Sandy said he didn't know but could guess. He had driven down with Norma, so Rob piled him in his car. Remus jumped into the backseat and lay down. The house was buzzing with the cousins' voices, sounding like a swarm of bees just deciding to hive.

Sandy protested all the way to town.

"They stretch that account to the limit. I cover up for them. Buying liquor. Paying off debts. I don't think they'd tell all that to Norma's dad."

Rob felt he'd never left Memphis, cleaning up behind Congressman Stockton. Not at all what he came for.

The town unfolded in its ancient way, up past the filling station, the drugstore, the courthouse, and on to dusty old Homestead Inn with its white columns needing paint and cracked brick walk, but inside nice and homey. The boy at reception looked up with a ready smile, but Rob waved him silent, while Sandy made a cautious circuit around the lobby and ducked into a passage back of the desk.

It opened into an office, with files ranked along one wall and two ample sofas cornered near a back window. On one of them a heavyset man sprawled at leisure. He sat his tall glass down beside the half-empty bourbon bottle and snorted with delight.

"If it ain't the bridegroom! Who's your friend?"

Rob got presented to Milton Ward, head of the road crew. There was a second man, sitting on the rug under the window, likewise nursing a tall glass of amber-colored drink. Jamie Hackett. Friday had come for them both.

"This is serious," Rob announced. His tone left no doubt. He refused a drink. "We've got to talk."

He sat on the vacant couch and bent forward. Jamie Hackett got up to listen. Milton Ward leaned closer. Sandy kept nodding agreement, but also stuck in his own comments. He hadn't thought it was serious to borrow a little. It had seemed like an emergency.

"Why in hell did I tell him?" Ward marveled at himself. "Just to watch out for this shyster here. It's all I said." He slapped Sandy on the shoulder. "It was a joke."

"You don't know Uncle Mack," Rob said. "He's got these Presbyterian ideas. He knows what sin is. He's always thinking about money. Also, he's a teetotaler. He might stop the whole show. They're already mad at Normie."

"That pretty girl? Why?"

"Her dress," Sandy explained. "She doesn't want to dress pretty."

"Well, that's easy," said Milton Ward. He had raised two daughters. "Just tell her she's got to."

"You don't know Norma," said Rob.

"Seems like I don't know anybody. So what you want from me?"

"Sober up," Rob advised. "Then get hold of Uncle Mack. Say it was all a mistake. Sandy's paid it back."

"I can't," said Sandy. "I got to have it. I paid for that suit. And Florida is coming up fast."

"We'll figure it out," Rob said, and wondered how much was in his bank account. Oh, those summers when he stayed with these kinfolks, paying nothing. Just freeloading, as they sometimes even told him, the mean ones, playing tennis or cards, shoving him aside. He was such a little squirt, one of them said. *You gonna ever grow up?* That was one of the bunch from Jackson, not close kin.

"We've got to get to the bank," Rob said, pushing Sandy toward the door.

"I'm due at the church pretty soon," Milton Ward said. "I'm the best man. What time is it?"

"Don't come drunk," Rob said. "Butter him up about Sandy. Lie if you have to."

"Not exactly lying. I owe this boy here a favor, don't I?"

"Lots of 'em," said Sandy, in a whisper.

A clutter of voices came from the lobby. *Oh Lord, the cousins,* thought Rob. "Is there some way out the back?"

There was.

He and Sandy found a door and sneaked out the back of the old hotel to the car. Nobody saw them.

Then the bank.

It was nearly four. Rob had read somewhere that four o'clock was the dead hour. If you could live through four o'clock you would get to another day. Rob reckoned he would make it, as after concluding the bank business, he dropped off Sandy and Remus. ("Can't you keep Remus?" Sandy asked. "No, I can't," said Rob.

Remus licked his face.) He drove to the house to catch his breath and get ready for dinner at the club.

◆

The house was quiet. He welcomed its peace and the chance to feel what he had come for, reflection and memories. There was a narrow stair, he recalled, leading up to a single large room, made from what was once the attic. In that room, his aunt had often sat with her sewing machine. She would bend forward to guide the cloth beneath the needle, turning it, stopping to release it, pushing it forward again. Again the clicking.

Sometimes alone with her he had sat on the floor near enough to lean against her and at times she would stop stitching and bend over to muss his hair. He might be discouraged at some way they had acted down below and she might know that without his saying anything because when she touched him, she would press him encouragingly and say "How's Rob? Bless your heart." He liked having his heart blessed.

The sewing machine was shoved back in a corner and looked sidetracked. He sat down on a couch and felt a breeze through the open window. Like a scent in the air, he thought of her as a mother.

But then he heard footsteps on the stair. Emily.

"Not at the church?" he asked.

"I didn't want to go. I'm not in it."

"Why not?"

"I had a fuss with Normie. I wanted to borrow her eye makeup but she wouldn't let me. I called her a bitch. Then she said I couldn't be in it. I said I didn't care."

She sat down on a stool.

"Aunt Alicia showed up, with Uncle Harry. They rented the big suite at the inn. They drove a Jaguar. It's long and shiny."

Rob said he imagined so. They sat silently. So much he could ask her . . . school . . . friends . . . parents . . . But she seemed content. A moth floated through the air and landed on the blind.

"I guess you've seen it," said Emily.

"Seen what?"

She got up, a slight girl, sturdy, getting grown-up looks. She moved to open a cupboard door, wanting him to look.

The dress, which was clothing a headless manikin, was white, ruffled and so sculpted to fit it appeared to have grown in place. Rob caught his breath at the sight, for it seemed all the weddings that had ever been were stated by it, and he felt Norma's presence glowing in its lines. He remembered his own modest wedding and his heart ached for all the hopes wrapped up in all weddings, everywhere in the world.

"Now she won't wear it," Emily said, and stood beside him. She stood on a level with him. On impulse from the dress, they turned and kissed.

◆

The swirl of getting to the dinner at the club drew them in, like the suction pipe at the gin. Dressing, racing, driving, then on through the doors at the country club. A rush of voices.

"Why Rob Ellis, come all this way!" He was hustled up to Aunt Alicia and Uncle Harry, who exclaimed over his job in politics and wanted to know . . . to know . . . know . . . Drink in hand, he tried to answer, to keep a light tone, say something funny. The very look of them said Important People. Aunt Alicia was not so much plump as stout, not so much stout as filling space. Her satiny outfit was handsome. Uncle Harry, thin beside her, wore the look of doing everything right. They had favored everyone by coming.

Uncle Mack was pulling him aside. "Say, you know? When I finally got to Milton Ward he said that was all a mistake about Sandy. If he borrowed it at all, it's been paid back. Maybe it was somebody else."

"It could be."

"Stockton called for you from Memphis. Wanted to talk to you . . . had to, he said."

"Said what about?"

"A speech. One of the clubs in Memphis. Rotary, I think he said."

"I better call back. He just needs a start-up, then he's off full speed."

"Important job you've got, old boy." Odd to be called that.

Across the room, Norma in discreet silk, smiled and chatted to the right, her arm hooked in Sandy's, while he talked to the left. But where was her mother? *Muzzy*, he thought.

"Why, Rob," he heard at his shoulder, almost in his ear. "If it isn't Rob. Bless your heart." And so she remembered. Or did she just bless everybody's heart? He gave his hug and took his kiss and looked into her eyes. They were a pale gray, not melting brown or declaring blue. What filled them was love, the kind of love just previous to tears. He all but wept himself.

In a last meeting his wife Doris had stood before him and said "I love you and I don't really want to go." It was only that they bored each other. They never had much to say. Her family never liked him. Did they like anybody? And then the quarrels set in. And the flirting. And the lies. But she stood there saying she loved him and not going anywhere. Until she did. His heart was not so much broken. He did not know what that was. What afflicted his heart, like a virus maybe, was yearning. *Please*, he would whisper to no one sometimes when he was alone, not quite knowing what he meant. He thought it now, then he drank enough to forget it.

◆

But where should he sleep? They forgot to tell him. Back at the house, he gravitated upstairs to the same old sewing room where he felt at home. He passed one of them below the stair and said, "Is this all right?" "Sure it is," was the answer. He climbed, laid down his small suitcase, and closed the door. He sat down and sighed. It had been a long day.

Minutes later, a tap at the door and he knew it wasn't over yet. He opened and found Norma standing there, holding a bottle and two glasses.

She sat down on the step, handed him a glass, and poured out whiskey.

"I was good at the dinner," she whispered. "I didn't have but one drink. I brought your old glass."

She had indeed. It was a heavy carved crystal glass, unlike any other, that Muzzy put aside for him long ago. Chocolate milk. Iced tea. Now whiskey.

"Won't they find us?"

"No. Everybody's too tired."

"So you conformed about likker," he teased her. "But not about the dress."

"The dress." She was suddenly quiet and serious.

"Nobody understands anything. How could I parade around in white? They all know I'm no shy little virgin. Except Muzzy. She never believes I do anything bad."

"She loves you. She made it for you."

"No she didn't. She had to get Miss Amy Johnson to do the ruffles. Miss Amy is expert. Twice before I almost got married. But we never made it to a dress with Pete and Horace."

He did not inquire about Pete and Horace. She rushed on.

"You remember the time when we were growing up and you were here for the summer? We put you in that trolley we had strung up between two trees. Halfway down it fell. If you hadn't tucked up your legs, they would have broken, half in two."

"I'd be even shorter. A midget."

"I was thinking the other day . . ." Off on the past. The games—tennis, cards—the picnics, the swims, the quarrels. How happy they had been. Protected, playing, arguing, safe. They hadn't known how lucky they were. As she spoke of it, he thought so too. Else what had he come back to discover? Another tilt from the bottle . . . He interrupted. "This glass. It used to be mine."

"I know," she said. "I brought it for you. We kept it. But why couldn't we keep those happy days?"

"They still want you to be happy. Your father told me. He cried."

"Daddy cried? Feature that."

"I saw the dress," he said.

She started. "How?"

"Emily showed me."

"Oh Lord, Emily . . . I want to wear what I want! I want it to state something. I want to say I'm my own person. I'm going to be happy again with Sandy, even if he's not from around here. Everybody will see it. I want to be myself! I want to say who *I am*!!" But in her excitement what she said came out like *jam*.

"Strawberry jam?" Rob inquired. They both fell to laughing. They laughed until they cried, they couldn't stop laughing.

"Are youall still up?" A voice from below. And there in the shadows Aunt Molly appeared in her long pale housecoat, a faintly glowing outline, like a spirit.

Norma leaned toward him, not to hug as he thought, but to hide the bottle. She left it and the glasses with him and teetered off down the stair.

◆

What a day! Rob's mind was fairly clear, and what pressed into it as Norma's tirade melted, was how Sandy had sought him out at the club, ambushed him in an alcove near the men's room. His face was strained with appeal, under the topping of thick blond hair, the eyes pleading.

"Do you know how much I thank you? This wouldn't have happened at all except for you. You saved me. I want you to know—

"It's okay."

"No, you have to realize. And of course I'll pay back, every cent. Soon's I can."

"I know. It's okay."

"You know why they looked at that account? It was Jamie Hackett. That guy you met at the hotel. He wanted to borrow some money. He got the boss to check the account. They saw where it had gone. Maybe I could have straightened it out somehow. But if it hadn't been for you—"

"It's okay."

◆

He slept, and suddenly it was morning. He remembered that he had to call Stockton, then go to the wedding.

On the way out he was waylaid by his cousin Marty. The old lady had the sleeve of her dress caught in her fine hair. He had to help untangle her, threads and hairs, one by one.

He went to the inn to call Stockton. The call was a long one. He barely made it to the church before Mendelssohn. And with the music there came Norma and Uncle Mack. She was wearing the white dress. Was it their laughter on the stair that had changed her? Or her mother's calling? Or her father's tears? Something had. Emily spread flowers in the aisle. She must have got the eye shadow. The little cousins who were bridesmaids looked solemn and exalted. Sandy, tame in his dark suit, discovered dignity.

Why had anyone worried?

The reception was held at the inn where once again Uncle Mack drew him aside.

"Rob, I think you must have helped that boy out."

He pretended puzzlement.

"I mean the one she just married. The Clemons boy at the bank gave me a clue."

Did nobody ever keep a promise not to tell? Rob wondered. They had all but pinned Al Clemons to the floor to swear him to silence.

"If you gave him anything, I want to pay you everything back. Every cent."

"Oh, no. Better talk to Sandy. He would know."

"I'm in the dark."

They were standing apart in an alcove room, meant for small dinners. Rob watched Uncle Mack as he stood reflecting over all he knew and what he didn't know. Uncle Mack liked control. Decision.

"Son," he said, "I know your father died not long ago and you got nobody left. But you got us. You got me for your father, and Molly for your mother, and Normie too and all the rest of us. But mainly me. I want you to call this home. It's a sacred word, son. It's yours."

So now at last, a father. The words struck through Rob's breast. Words from an honest man who meant what he said. There were none who ever doubted him, none he ever failed. *Did I come for this?*

◆

Leaving time. He had promised Stockton he would drive back that very night. Storing his bag in the car, he checked to see if by any chance Remus was in the backseat.

He drove out in the late afternoon. He passed the orange-colored monsters of the road construction, towering over the old hills now crumbled, shaping into a highway that would sweep thoughtlessly past the little town of his youth.

He fell to wondering what he had come here and done. His bank account was considerably diminished. Had he secured the marriage of a possible alcoholic to a possible crook? But he remembered the scene beneath the pecan trees and refused a dark scenario. He held to the warmth of his uncle's words. They grew like a firm standing place beneath his feet.

At the reception, Emily had crept closer. She had squeezed his hand. He felt he could come back to her. But courting cousins wouldn't work.

The miles fled beneath him. "You're going with me to Washington, son," Stockton had said. "It will be a whole new world."

Acknowledgments

I wish to give special thanks for help and encouragement to Allan Gurganus, Louis Rubin, Margie and Terry Roberts, Sally Greene, and Sharon Swanson. Also to members of our monthly writers group, which includes Walter Bennett, Lewis Lipsitz, and others, willing listeners and critics whose comments aided me so much, and to all the warm friends of Chapel Hill, North Carolina, our special home.

—Elizabeth Spencer

Credits

"Return Trip." (First published in *Five Points*.) Most recently published in *New Stories from the South: The Year's Best, 2010*. Algonquin Books of Chapel Hill, a Division of Workman Publishing Company (January 2010).

"The Boy in the Tree." (First published in *The Southern Review* 40.3.) Most recently published in *New Stories from the South: The Year's Best, 2005*. Algonquin Books of Chapel Hill, a Division of Workman Publishing Company (November 2004).

"Sightings." *The Hudson Review* (July 2008).

"Rising Tide." *The Oxford American* (July 2010).

"The Everlasting Light." (Originally published by *Raleigh News & Observer* 1998. Also appears in *The Cry of an Occasion: Fiction from the Fellowship of Southern Writers*, 2001.) Most recently published in *Long Story Short; Flash Fiction by 65 of North Carolina's Finest Writers*. University of North Carolina Press (February 2009).

"On the Hill." *Five Points 15.1&2*. Georgia State University Press (February 2013).

"Blackie." *Epoch Magazine 61.1*. Cornell University Press (2012 Series).

"Christmas Longings." *Our State* (December 2012).

"The Wedding Visitor." *ZYZZYVA* (July 2013).

About the Author

Elizabeth Spencer was born in Carrollton, Mississippi. She received an MA from Vanderbilt University in 1943. Her first novel, *Fire in the Morning*, was published in 1948; eight other novels followed, as well as stories that appeared in *The New Yorker*, *The Atlantic*, and other magazines.

Spencer went to Italy in 1953 on a Guggenheim Fellowship, where she met her future husband, John Rusher. In 1986 they moved to Chapel Hill, where she taught writing at the University of North Carolina until 1992.

Previous to *Starting Over*, her most recent book is *The Southern Woman: New and Selected Fiction*. Other titles include *The Voice at the Back Door*, *The Salt Line*, and *The Night Travellers*.

The Light in the Piazza, first published in *The New Yorker* in 1960 and then as a novella in the same year, was made into a movie in 1963. Four decades later, in 2005, it premiered as a Broadway musical and won six Tony Awards in June 2006.

Spencer's writing has received numerous awards, including the Award of Merit from the American Academy of Arts and Letters, the PEN/Malamud Award for Short Fiction, and the Lifetime Achievement Award from the Mississippi Institute of Arts and Letters. She is a member of the American Academy of Arts and Letters and a charter member of the Fellowship of Southern Writers.

A documentary film has been produced on her life and work entitled *Landscapes of the Heart: The Elizabeth Spencer Story*.